G. B. Gurland has been an educator for over forty years. She has extensive experience working with children, adolescents, and young adults with reading and literacy challenges. She has edited and published several workbooks in the area of vocabulary development, and is the author of the highly praised middle grade novel, *The Secret Files of Phineas Foster*, as well as the delightful *Olives, Where Are You?*, and *Emily Fisher-Word Maven* for young readers.

For Sharon, mother, grandmother, and great grandmother,
whose imagination and wit will inspire storytelling
for generations.

G. B. Gurland

ORPHAN'S BOND

AUSTIN MACAULEY PUBLISHERS™

LONDON · CAMBRIDGE · NEW YORK · SHARJAH

Ordering Information
Quantity sales: Special discounts are available on quantity purchases by corporations, associations, and others. For details, contact the publisher at the address below.

Publisher's Cataloging-in-Publication data
Gurland, G. B.
Orphan's Bond

ISBN 9781647501976 (Paperback)
ISBN 9781647501983 (ePub e-book)

Library of Congress Control Number: 2020920220

www.austinmacauley.com/us

First Published (2021)
Austin Macauley Publishers LLC
40 Wall Street, 33rd Floor, Suite 3302
New York, NY 10005
USA

mail-usa@austinmacauley.com
+1 (646) 5125767

Thank you to those who encouraged me to write this story and trusted me enough to read it. My heartfelt appreciation to the children who accompanied me on this journey, asked questions when things did not quite make sense, and prodded me for the next chapter. I know of no more skilled editors and exacting critics than Emily and Rebecca, or engaged readers than Noah and Bracha. My deepest respect for all of the children's authors I have met through Gotham Writers Workshop and the Society for Children's Book Writers and Illustrators, most notably Harriet Hyman Alonso, Lizzie Ross, Laurin Grollman, and Joe Nagler. I am indebted to family, friends, and colleagues who read, commented, and encouraged me along the way: Dara, Bradley and Lauren Adler, Sharon Modell, Andrea Blau, Susan Bohne, Leda Molly, Rochelle Roth, Bob Scherma, Dorothy Varon, and Sylvia Walters. It is a daunting responsibility to bring characters to the page and tell their story. I could easily have abandoned that undertaking if not for the boundless love and support of Beryl Adler.

Table of Contents

Chapter One
Speechless

Now I feel like a complete idiot. Of course, Grandpa can't talk. What a moron I am. Half his brain is fried because of that stroke. But there is something he wanted to tell me, something important. At least that's what he said when he phoned last night and asked me to stop by his house after school today.

I pace up and down the emergency room, waiting for my parents to finish with the doctors. It seems like forever since they disappeared behind the doorway marked **AUTHORIZED PERSONNEL, DO NOT ENTER.**

I see my brother's khaki jacket and red scarf before I hear him.

"Hey, Robbie," Henry calls out. He struts down the hallway in his characteristically cocky way.

I don't think I have ever been happier to see my big brother. That is until he opens his mouth again. "Is he dead? When Mom told me to drop everything and get here, I figured he was dead."

"He's not dead!" I shout. "Don't be such a jerk, Henry. He had a stroke. He's paralyzed and he can't talk, but he's not dead!"

"Chill out, Robbie. I know he meant a lot to you. It's just that he never had too much to say to me even before this happened."

"Means a lot to me, not meant, Henry. Stop talking about Grandpa in the past tense."

"Okay, okay, where are Mom and Dad, anyway?" Henry asks.

"The doctors came out to get them about 15 minutes ago. They said I had to wait here."

We don't speak to each other after that typically disagreeable encounter. I sit on one end of the row of hard plastic seats, and Henry sits on the other. He barely puts his phone down for more than a few seconds. If texting were an Olympic event, there is no doubt Henry would be a gold medalist.

I pull out a book from my backpack—yes, indeed a book, the kind with pages made of paper. No luck though, I can't concentrate, not even for a few seconds. I jump up every time I hear footsteps. Doctors and nurses enter and exit. Carts rattle as they are wheeled back and forth. I glance repeatedly at my watch as if that will make the time pass more quickly. It is at least another half hour before my parents finally emerge from behind the forbidden doorway.

"Oh, thank heavens you're here, Henry," Mom blurts out. Figures, big brother gets the hero's welcome once again. He stays away as long as he likes, swoops in like the prince, and Mom lays out the red carpet for him, *her he can do no wrong son, Henry*!

"Mom, how's Grandpa? Can I see him now?" I ask.

"Not yet, Robbie. He's had a pretty serious stroke and isn't very responsive as yet. He's stable, but the doctors want him to rest as much as possible. Even when he's awake, he only makes some grunting sounds. They say he has something called aphasia, which basically means he can't talk and may not even understand what we say to him," Mom explains.

"But he'll get better. There must be medicines or therapy or something that will help him get better, right?" I speak these words, only partly convinced of what I'm saying and mostly pleading for Grandpa's recovery. He has to speak again. He has more stories to tell me and something that is important enough for him to ask me to come over after school today by myself.

Grandpa was very clear, "Robbie, I need to tell you something. You remember that story about my old neighborhood, the one about the art dealer who lived in the apartment next door. There's more I need to tell you. But not now, in person, tomorrow after school."

That was it. That is all I know, and then we get a call in the middle of the night from one of these alarm companies that keep track of old people. Mom wakes me up.

"Grandpa's been rushed to the hospital. They think he had a stroke. I'm heading over there now. You get dressed and come with Dad. Henry is driving back from college. I'm so grateful he's coming home to be with us. It will be such a relief to have him here."

Grandpa is lying in the emergency room, more dead than alive. Sure Mom is worried, but if you ask me, the real big deal for her is the return of *Prince Henry*. Funny what flunking out of two schools, a near drug overdose, and a stint in rehab can do to keep you front and center in your

15

parents' minds. Equally funny how being a top student and basic nerd can get you taken for granted.

But not by Grandpa. Maybe it is because I was named after him. Henry was named after my paternal grandfather; I was named after my maternal grandfather. At least our first and middle names are the same. Grandpa, of course, is John Robert Orphan; I'm John Robert O'Neill. No one would ever think of calling Grandpa anything other than John; I have always been known as Robbie.

I am the kind of kid every parent hopes for and then mostly overlooks. I stay out of trouble and get good grades. I'm not big on sports. And while admitting this doesn't exactly help me win friends and influence people—at least people in the seventh grade—I love to hang out with my grandfather. He tells about the best stories of anyone. I'm not sure they're all true, even though he swears they are. And now what? He may never speak again.

"Robbie, Henry's going to drive you home so Dad and I can stay here in case Grandpa wakes up and we can see him. I don't know what we would do without your big brother. It's so comforting to have him home with us in the middle of all this."

I think I will barf now. Mom may be comforted by Henry's return. I'll just be happy if he gets me home in one piece.

"Don't look so glum, little brother. Come on, I'll buy you some breakfast on the way to the house."

I follow Henry down the hospital corridor to the parking lot when my cell phone rings. I don't recognize the incoming number and let the call go to voicemail. Henry and I barely speak on the ride home. We never do stop for breakfast. He pulls into the driveway, checks to see if I have the key, and takes off. Yes, it is very comforting to have my big brother back home.

I unlock the door, take off my jacket, pour myself a glass of OJ, and listen to the voicemail on my cell. It's some girl's voice. She sounds like she could be around the same age as me, maybe older. "This message is for Robbie O'Neill. Your grandfather asked me to call you if I couldn't reach him. He said I could trust you. I'll call you again later. Your grandfather will explain."

Chapter Two
Grandpa's Stuff

Grandpa has a million and one stories, not just about the old neighborhood. Some of them were handed down from his parents, my great-grandparents. Harrowing escapes in the middle of the night from Russian labor camps, relatives shot in the head by marauding soldiers on horseback, disease, famine. He could make the Old and New Testament seem boring by comparison.

Not all of his stories were quite so dramatic. Some of them were downright funny. There was the one about being late for his first day at work. He was so busy making sure his tie was straight, he never looked down to see he had forgotten to put his pants on. He figured it out by the time he got to the bus stop, but not before the kids on the block nicknamed him *Legs*. Some he told over and over again, each time with a slightly different ending. He never tired of telling them, and I never tired of hearing them.

"Grandpa, you should write a book one of these days."

"Yeah, yeah, you write the book for me, Robbie. I'm good at talking. You're the writer."

He was good at talking, and that's the operative word, *was*. Now, he might never speak again.

I was up most of the night and in no shape to go to school. There goes my perfect attendance record. Big deal, I have more important matters to handle. I take a shower and wait to hear from Mom or Dad. Who knows, maybe *Prince Henry* will return with some news. Or maybe, the girl who left the voicemail earlier will call again.

The phone does ring, but it's no one I'm hoping to hear from. "Hey Robbie, how come you're not in school today? We're supposed to hand in the science fair project and it's in the trunk of your mother's car."

"Oh shoot, sorry Zach. I can't go into the whole thing, but my grandfather was rushed to the hospital last night, and everything's pretty much a disaster right now. Just explain things to Mr. Cooper, and I'll figure something out by tomorrow."

I get off the phone with Zach as fast as I can. I can't think about science projects at a time like this. I hear the crunch of gravel as the car pulls into the driveway. Within seconds, Dad steps through the doorway, carrying a large plastic bag.

"Mom is staying at the hospital in case Grandpa wakes up. It's not looking too good. Grandpa is in pretty bad shape. Even if he gets through this, he's going to need round the clock nursing care. He's not going to be the same, Robbie," Dad explains.

Once we clear up that Henry left as soon as he dropped me off, and Dad spares us both making some lame excuse to explain his elder son's absence, I finally just break down and have the cry I've been holding in for hours. Dad does his best to comfort me, but he can't quite conceal his own emotions. He always had a special connection to Grandpa, particularly since his own father died last year.

When we both get ourselves a bit more together, I ask Dad about the plastic bag, "Are those Grandpa's things? Where'd they come from?"

"It seems Grandpa was wearing his old down parka when he collapsed, almost as if he were heading out somewhere in the middle of the night. You know the jacket, Robbie, the one with the gazillion pockets. The emergency room staff asked us to empty all of the pockets and take his personal belongings home. I just filled up this plastic bag and figured Mom and I would look through everything later. Have a look if you want to. I'm going to shower and change my clothes."

I want to look. I don't want to look. It seems like an invasion of privacy. But that is weird. Why did Grandpa have his jacket on in the middle of the night? Where could he possibly have been going?

I stare at the bag, hoping that the transparent plastic will give me a reason to investigate further. I'm able to make out a worn brown leather wallet, keys, a few forbidden stray cigarettes, disposable lighter, gloves, checkbook, cell phone, and several envelopes held together with a rubber band.

The bag begins to vibrate as the cell phone inside sounds off. That is the excuse I need, the invitation I want. I fumble with the metal tie that holds the bag closed, but reach the phone too late. The number of the missed call flashes on the screen. It is the same caller who left the voicemail message for me that morning.

As soon as I place the phone back in the plastic bag and reseal it, my cell rings. The now-familiar caller ID appears on the screen. "Hello," I say cautiously.

"Is this John Robert Orphan's grandson Robbie?" the soft-spoken caller asks tentatively.

"It is," I respond, but abruptly hang up as my big brother barges into the kitchen.

"Who are you talking to, Robbie, and what's with the plastic bag?"

"A friend from school, and leave the bag alone, Henry. Dad brought it home from the hospital. It's Grandpa's stuff so keep your grubby hands off of it."

"Okay, little brother. I know you're upset about the old man, but you don't have to be so touchy."

"Stop calling him an old man, and I'm not being touchy. It's just that it's Grandpa's private stuff and we have no business going through it."

"Yeah, like you weren't about to open the bag and check it out," Henry says accusingly.

Dad walks in just in time because I have about all I can take of Henry at the moment. Dad has just gotten off the phone with Mom and brings the first good news of the day. Grandpa is awake and alert. He still isn't talking, but somehow through the gestures and grunts, he managed to let Mom know he wants to see me.

Dad has to go into the office for a few hours so I am again at the mercy of Henry, who couldn't be happier with the excuse this gives him not to return to school for a few days. Dad leaves, and Henry and I get into his car. We don't say a word to each other on the drive back to the hospital. As for the plastic bag, that remains unexamined on the kitchen counter. I still feel weird about going through Grandpa's stuff, but there are some very strange things happening. I don't think I'll get much out of Grandpa in his condition, but if I can get a few minutes alone, I might be able to phone the number on my caller ID.

Chapter Three
A Stroke of Luck

Mom cautions me about keeping the visit short. She tells me that even if Grandpa tries to speak, it is likely to sound garbled and not mean much. The doctor says this is pretty typical and that the next several days will determine just how much of his speech will come back.

"Mom, I'm scared. Are you sure he'll know who I am?"

"He seems to recognize everyone, and he made himself pretty clear. He wants to see you. Just try not to tire him out or let him get frustrated. If you ask him yes/no questions, he'll respond by shaking his head. It's just that if he tries to speak, it won't make any sense to you."

I don't think I ever have been more nervous in my life. I want to see Grandpa more than anything. But I don't dare mention why he wanted to see me or ask about the nameless caller.

Mom and I walk down the corridor from the waiting room to the intensive care unit. We bump into nurses parading back and forth between the glass-enclosed rooms, as others stare at monitors, tracking patients' vital signs. There is an eerie silence, broken only by the clicks and beeps of the medical equipment that surrounds us.

"Do you want me to come in with you, Robbie?" Mom inquires.

"I think I can do this. Just wait out here for me, Mom."

Grandpa opens his eyes as I enter the room and approach his bed. He reaches for me with his left hand, as his right arm lays motionless next to him. His smile twists unexpectedly to one side of his face. Yet, it is most definitely a sign that he is pleased to see me.

Just stick with yes/no questions Robbie, I tell myself.

"Can I give you a hug, Grandpa?" Affirmative.

"Are you feeling better?" Affirmative.

"Are the doctors taking good care of you?" Affirmative.

Okay, that is all pretty safe and doesn't seem to upset him.

He glances at the chair next to the bed. I follow the signal as best as I can. He begins to utter a series of sounds, which, as I was warned, are meaningless to me, but clearly not to him. Grandpa is trying to tell me something, and he isn't giving up until he succeeds.

Okay, keep it simple Robbie, I remind myself. Go back to the yes/no questions.

"Were you going out last night when you collapsed?" Negative.

"But you had your jacket on?" Affirmative.

"If you weren't going out, were you coming back home?" Affirmative

"Did you meet someone last night?" Affirmative.

This isn't going so badly after all, until we hit another roadblock of jumbled syllables. While they seem to make total sense to Grandpa, I don't understand a word.

Get back on safe ground, Robbie. But there are just so many yes/no questions I can ask. I want to know who, where, and why. Grandpa is losing patience and getting frustrated. The last thing I want to do is stress him out. But I take a chance and ask him.

"Do you know who has been trying to call me?" Affirmative.

"It sounded like a kid's voice. A girl." Affirmative.

"Is she someone you know, Grandpa?" No response. I thought that was a pretty safe yes/no question, but he just looks up at the ceiling and stares.

That is about the end of the line for me. I have no idea where to go next. Mom pokes her head in to see if everything is all right.

"Robbie, is Grandpa okay? He seems a bit agitated. Maybe that's enough for now. You can visit again later or tomorrow."

There is no mistaking Grandpa's response this time. Negative, negative, negative!

"Just let me have a few more minutes, Mom."

"Okay Robbie, but he's not supposed to get worked up, and he needs his rest," Mom repeats as she slowly backs out of the doorway.

Another series of meaningless grunts, and then suddenly a word, a syllable, a string of syllables I can almost understand. "Te, tefo, nu, nu, num."

"Do you want me to call the girl back?" Affirmative.

No point asking who she is. There is no way I will understand him. I have an idea. I reach for my phone, put it close to his ear, and play the voicemail for Grandpa. His smile—misshapen and leaning to one side of his face—is undeniable. Something about the voice of the caller, known or unknown to Grandpa, makes him very happy.

"Okay, that's enough, guys," Mom interrupts as she steps inside the room. "Robbie, you've got to let Grandpa get some rest."

His smile retreats, yet he seems quite satisfied with himself. He closes his eyes and drifts into sleep. Grandpa has gotten his message across, perhaps more clearly than he might have with words. I still don't have a clue who this girl is, but I understand my task. I have to return her call.

Chapter Four
The Girl

I have no idea how I am going to get any time alone. I just know I have to make that phone call. With Grandpa not able to tell me much more, I have to find out who that girl is and what she knows about my grandfather.

I glance at Mom who looks completely exhausted. "Mom, you look wrecked."

"I was up most of the night, Robbie. I caught a few catnaps, but I'm pretty worn out."

"Grandpa is stable for now, and I don't think much is going to change in the next few hours, Mom. Why don't you go home, get some rest, and shower? I'll hang out here and promise to call if anything happens."

"What about school, Robbie? You never miss school."

"Well, I guess there's a first time for everything. This waiting room looks like a pretty safe place for me to hang out. And Dad will be back as soon as he checks on the office. I'm good Mom, trust me," I assure her.

"I trust you, Robbie. It's everyone else I worry about. Let me call Henry and have him come back here to stay with you," Mom offers.

Just what I need, Henry! But I sure can't burst Mom's *Prince Henry, the Savior* bubble, not now anyway. She has her fantasy about my big brother, and I'm not going to take that away from her, not today.

"You know what Mom, you get going. I'll call Henry. I'm sure he'll get back here in no time. I'll be just fine until he shows up."

She does it. I can tell she is not too comfortable with the idea, but she actually leaves me here by myself. I have the opening I need. I'm sure not about to call Henry, at least not right away, not that he would come rushing back. I grab my phone and press call back from the voicemail message.

I take a deep breath and wait. Three, four, five rings— no answer. Finally a recording, but not the girl's voice. It is an older woman, with an accent, maybe Russian or German.

I hang up. I'm not sure why, but something just makes me hang up. I have no clue what to say. *This is John Robert Orphan's grandson*—that is dumb! *You've been trying to call me*—that is even dumber! I have no idea who I am even trying to call and the older voice just throws me.

And then the phone rings. It is the same number I just called. It is the girl's voice. "Robbie, is that you? I've been trying to reach you."

"This is Robbie O'Neill, John Robert Orphan's grandson. Who are you?"

"I'll get to that in just a second, that is if you don't hang up on me again," the girl replies.

"Sorry about that. It's just that this whole thing has been kind of weird," I say a bit more politely.

"Well, it's been pretty weird for me too. I just found out about your grandfather a few days ago."

"Found out what exactly? Who are you?" I insist.

"My name is Rebecca, Rebecca Bauer."

That is about all she tells me on the phone. So now I know the girl's name, and that she knows something about my grandfather. That is it, at least until we can meet. And she doesn't want to meet just anywhere. When I tell her my grandfather had a stroke and is in ICU, she insists on coming to the hospital. It takes all my powers of persuasion to convince her it's a bad idea.

We can't come up with an alternative, at least one that doesn't involve my parents finding out about this just yet. And that is one thing she is pretty clear about. My parents have to be kept out of this for now. According to Rebecca, that was my grandfather's wish when he found out about the letter. What letter? She won't say, at least not over the phone. And then she hangs up.

I try to call her back when I spot Dad walking toward me. I stuff the phone into my backpack and do the best I can to seem cool. But on the inside, I am anything but cool. And I can't say anything—not to him, not to Mom, and not to Grandpa—unless I can figure out a way to get back into his room and start the yes/no question game again.

"Mom told me Henry was coming back to hang out with you. Where is he?" Dad asks.

Is it time for a little white lie or true confessions? Dad is a bit more of a realist than Mom when it comes to Henry, but I go with the lie, the first of many I will tell in the next several days, thanks to the appearance of Rebecca Bauer.

"I tried to call Henry after Mom left, but I must have the wrong number. I got some strange voicemail message and figured I would just wait until you got back from the office."

Dad is pretty savvy and I'm not sure that he buys it. He has that certain look in his eyes, but for the moment, he doesn't say anything else, at least about Henry or the phone call. I wait while he walks over to one of the nurses. They speak briefly, and he motions for me to follow him back into Grandpa's room.

As we enter the room, Grandpa seems more alert this time. The machines and tubes are still a bit scary, but I've gotten used to the half smile and fragments of words by now. I just want to get him alone for a few more minutes to see if there is anything else I might learn about the girl on the phone—if the yes/no questions will yield any more information.

Dad makes some reassuring small talk about the doctors and nurses and how well Grandpa is doing. We are asked to step out when the speech therapist arrives for some sort of bedside evaluation. Grandpa falls asleep. Mom shows up, followed by Henry. It seems like hours have passed, and I am about to lose it.

My phone rings and the now-familiar caller ID appears on the screen. Lie number two. I tell my parents Zach called to leave a message about school and the science project. Mom declares that both the science project and I will be delivered to school tomorrow. Now I am really going out of my mind. Grandpa is 20 feet away and unreachable; the girl, I mean Rebecca, is trying to call me again, and I am surrounded by the entire O'Neill clan.

The meal trays are wheeled in for whichever patients in ICU are able to eat. The speech therapist ordered a soft diet for Grandpa, which means he gets a tray, and I get a break. The nurse doesn't think it is a great idea for us all to hover

over Grandpa while he tries to eat. She asks him who he wants to help him. I get the nod and the now-familiar skewed smile.

"Okay, we'll wait outside," Mom announces. "Are you good with this, Robbie?"

I have my chance to be alone with Grandpa again and no idea what to do next. "I'm great, Mom!"

Chapter Five
The Letter

The good news is that I am alone with Grandpa. The bad news is that I have no idea how to get any more information from him about Rebecca. Mom thinks she is being inconspicuous as she paces back and forth outside of Grandpa's room. Dad and Henry are out of sight for the moment, probably sneaking a forbidden smoke, their one shared vice.

I look down at the bowl of mush that is trying to pass for dinner. Grandpa doesn't even wait for the question.

Negative! He is not eating this stuff.

"I don't blame you, Grandpa. But you've gotta try something or you'll make me look bad. And besides, wouldn't you rather deal with me than Mom?" Affirmative!

I fill the spoon and place it gently between Grandpa's lips. He manages to get a few mouthfuls down. Apparently, it tastes better than it looks. And then we both get tearful. The reversal of roles escapes neither of us. We know exactly what we're each thinking. We always do. He needs me to look after him now, like all of the times he has looked after me. That is one tough spot for a man like him to be in and one new reality I'm not sure I know how to handle.

He reaches for me with his remaining good arm, takes hold of my hand, and speaks paragraphs without uttering a word. The silence is brief and is followed by the most knowing of lopsided smiles. Grandpa needs my help. There is something he needs me to do for him, but what?

I know time is short and that Mom will burst into the room any second now to inspect and verify my progress with Grandpa's dinner. I slip the uneaten food into the trash, which produces Grandpa's first actual giggle. No sooner do I manage this maneuver than Mom appears. She seems a bit suspicious but lets it slide, much to my relief.

"Thanks, Robbie. My turn now. Can I have a few minutes with Grandpa?"

"Sure thing, Mom. I'll wait outside. I need to check in with Zach anyway about school tomorrow."

Lie number three. It's not Zach I intend to call. I have to try to reach Rebecca again. If I can't get anything else tonight from Grandpa about Rebecca, then I will see what else I can find out about Grandpa from her.

I make my way back to the waiting area through the maze of closely monitored cubicles. I get turned around for a second as a crowd of white coats and green scrubs responds to a code. Someone is definitely dying at the other end of the floor. I step out of the way and bump into a nurse who is not too happy about the charts I manage to knock out of her hands. She accepts my offer to help collect the airborne papers. I apologize and head for the door.

Dad and Henry are still nowhere in sight. I know Mom is going to stay with Grandpa for as long as the nurses let her. This is my chance. I check the old voicemail message and press call back again. This time, someone answers. It's a girl's voice.

"Robbie, is that you? Where are you?"

"I'm still in the hospital, and I still don't know anything more than your name."

"How is your grandfather?"

"He's doing a little better, but why do you even care? And what is this letter you were talking about before?" I ask impatiently.

"I would really prefer to explain all of this to you in person. Is there any way we can meet later today or tomorrow?"

"Are you kidding? I'm under surveillance 24/7, particularly now with my grandfather in the hospital. Any move I make is going to be tracked by my parents, particularly my mother. Why don't you just tell me what is going on?" I insist.

"Your grandfather asked me not to until he had a chance to speak with you first."

"Well, that's not going to happen any time soon. I know he was planning to tell me something, maybe something about you or this letter. But with the stroke, he can hardly string two syllables together. And when he does, it doesn't make a whole lot of sense. The ball is in your court, Rebecca, whoever you are. Grandpa can't tell me much more about you, so why don't you tell me what you know about him."

I continue to make my case when it gets really quiet on the other end. For a minute, I think she's hung up on me.

"Okay, okay. I can't tell you about the letter," Rebecca finally answers. "But I can show it to you. It's just that I don't know if that will make things clearer or even more confusing."

"We can't meet, not without getting my parents into the middle of this," I remind her.

"Don't worry. I'll figure out how to get it to you," Rebecca reassures me.

"Do you know where I live?" I ask.

"No, but I have an old address for your grandfather. It's on an envelope of a letter made out to him," Rebecca explains.

"If it was addressed to my grandfather, why wasn't it ever sent?"

"It was, but it was stamped *addressee unknown* and returned, unopened," she explains.

"What address was it sent to?" I ask.

"120 Garfield Place, Brooklyn, New York."

"When?" I continue.

"The letter is postmarked December 28, 1962. It was sent to a J. R. Bauer in care of John Robert Orphan over 50 years ago."

"From who?"

"From Nathan Bauer, your grandfather's brother."

"First, my grandfather's last name is not Bauer, and he doesn't have a brother or a sister. Second, he hasn't lived in Brooklyn for more than 50 years."

"I realize that, but his real name is Bauer. And he did have a brother," Rebecca insists. "My grandfather died two months ago, and that's when I found the letter in his attic. It's taken me all this time to find John Robert Orphan, alias Bauer. He does a pretty good job of covering his tracks. And when you read the letter, maybe you'll understand why."

Chapter Six
Only Child

You know how you're supposed to make a wish when you blow out your birthday candles. Well, I always have the same wish—that I am an only child. I know that sounds pretty awful, but it's not half as bad as having Henry for a brother.

We're seven years apart. Henry was planned and I was the accident. Maybe that is where my insecurity started. All those ideas about the youngest kid getting all of the attention—just a myth. Sure my parents loved me. I was little, cute and obedient—what's not to love? I think that was the problem. I was too obedient, and when I stopped being little and cute, it was all Henry, all the time.

Henry and I did okay at the beginning. But when I started to think for myself and realized he had turned me into his personal slave, it all went downhill. Year after year of me being on student honor roll didn't help our relationship either, not when the only reason your parents get called up to school is to negotiate the number of days of your suspension.

The one who gets me the best is Grandpa. He calls me an *old soul.* Neither of us understands Henry. I mean that literally. It's almost impossible to make any sense out of most of what he says.

Grandpa calls Henry *a work in progress.* I think he is just a lot of work. He is an absolute slob, wouldn't recognize a book if it hit him over the head, and worst of all, he has never kept a promise—not to me, not to Dad, and especially not to Mom. That's why I don't get this hero-worship thing she has going on with him. The more he disappoints her, the more she defends him, time and time again.

Grandpa says he always wanted a brother and that it was lonely growing up an only child. That's why I am convinced that Rebecca has this all wrong. How can Rebecca's grandfather, Nathan Bauer, be Grandpa's brother? That is not something he would keep from me. We tell each other everything. All those stories and never any mention of a brother, never! So who is John Robert Bauer?

I have to get my hands on that letter. Rebecca has a plan. It involves Rebecca, me, and Sherlock Holmes. It seems Rebecca's search has revealed Grandpa's current address, which coincidence or not, is not far from where she now lives with her grandmother. Why is she living with her grandmother? It has something to do with her parents and house hunting in California.

Rebecca makes a point of telling me she is not too fond of the suburbs, having grown up in Manhattan. Remaining east with her grandmother allows her to commute and graduate from her old school, some fancy shmancy private middle school in Riverdale. I go to public school, which I guess explains why we've never run into each other before.

"You know the public library, the one on Wilmott Street, off of Sixth?" Rebecca asks.

"Yeah, it's about three blocks from my school. I go there all the time when Mom needs me to wait until she can pick me up after school," I reply.

"Can you get there tomorrow after school?"

"I guess so. Why?"

Rebecca issues a very specific set of directions for me to follow. "Go there tomorrow afternoon. Ask the librarian for *The Complete Collection of Sherlock Holmes*. Open the book to *The Red-Headed League*. The letter will be there."

"And what if someone else gets to the book before me?" I wonder aloud.

"No worries. No one has borrowed that book in ages. Trust me. It will be there and so will the letter."

"And where will you be?" I ask.

"Long gone. I promise!" Rebecca replies.

I'm not sure what all of this cloak and dagger stuff is about. I just know I have to see what the deal is with this letter and if there is any possibility that Rebecca is on to something about Grandpa.

Mom says there will be no visiting Grandpa tomorrow until after school, anyway. She insists that I am not missing another day of school and that she will pick me up at the library as usual. The science project is in the trunk of the car. Zach has gotten Mr. Cooper to give us an extension. So far, so good. I just need to keep it together for the next 24 hours.

Mom is staying at the hospital through dinner tonight, so it's just Dad, Henry, and me. With Henry home, we're back to sharing a room. I take a deep breath and prepare for the usual chaos that accompanies my big brother wherever he goes. We order pizza. Zach calls with my make-up homework. Dad takes care of some office work. Things are going along okay until Henry brings up the plastic bag.

"Hey Pop, did you get a chance to look through that plastic bag you brought home from the hospital? You know, the one with Grandpa's things," Henry asks.

"Not yet. I thought I would leave that up to your mother."

"It was kind of weird, the old man going somewhere in the middle of the night. Maybe there's a hint about where he was going. Let's take a look. Mom will be cool with it."

"I think we should wait for Mom," I blurt out.

"Oh, there you go again little bro, like you weren't about to sneak a peek yesterday when I caught you in the act."

"I guess it wouldn't do any harm," Dad says.

These are the moments when my *only child* fantasies kick into full gear. I know Grandpa was not going out when he collapsed. He was returning from somewhere, and there is a good chance that the "somewhere" has something to do with Rebecca Bauer.

I'm pretty uneasy about the library, Sherlock Holmes, and the letter. I have to keep Henry away from the plastic bag. Desperate times call for desperate measures!

Lie number four. "The plastic bag isn't in the house anymore. It's in Mom's car," I interrupt. "She said she wants to go through Grandpa's things with him at the hospital tonight in case there is something he needs."

Actually, the bag is in the laundry room with some clean pajamas that Mom prepared to bring to the hospital if they transfer Grandpa to a regular room and let him change out of the hospital gown. There is no way Henry will go

39

anywhere near the laundry room, and with Dad busy with the office, I have the few minutes I need to find a place to hide the bag.

Henry takes up residence on the living room couch. The TV is blasting and he is plugged into his phone. If I luck out, he will fall asleep and stay down here for the night. If I really luck out, one of his charming friends will call him and he'll leave for a few hours. In any case, I have some breathing room to deal with the bag.

I grab the bag from the laundry room and put it in my backpack for now. Do I look through it or not? It still seems creepy to go through Grandpa's stuff. But things are different now. Not my room, the kitchen, or the garage—someone is bound to come poking around.

Lie number five. I knock on Dad's door. "Dad, I'm going over to Zach's house for a little while. We need to practice this thing we're presenting for science tomorrow."

"Okay, but please be home before your mother gets back. I don't want to give her anything else to worry about."

"Sure thing, Dad. I'll be back in an hour."

I take my bike and start riding. I don't have a clue where I'm going. I'll just know when I get there. Why didn't I think of this before? Grandpa's house! Nobody will ever look for me there. There is usually a key under the back doormat. Let's hope it is still there.

Chapter Seven
Three Paintings

It seems my bike and I are on the same wavelength. Once I decide where I'm going, it's like I'm on automatic pilot. North on Vanderbilt for six blocks, a right turn on Jefferson for three blocks, and left onto Dorchester for three more, until I reach 699.

I pull my bike up the driveway to the back and park it so that it is out of sight. The last thing I need is some nosy neighbor spotting me and poking around to see what's happening. Fortunately, Grandpa has never gotten around to fixing the sensor on the back porch light, which gives me the cover of darkness I need. There is just about enough light from my phone to find my way to the back door and the key under the doormat.

I unlock the door and try my best to do what I have to do without turning the lights on. I navigate my way through the kitchen down the hallway to Grandpa's room and settle myself on the floor next to his bed. I remove the plastic bag with Grandpa's things from my backpack. I'm not feeling too good about going through his stuff, but my curiosity is definitely getting the better of me. I open the bag and reach for the cell phone, the wallet, the checkbook, and the pack of rubber-banded envelopes.

The cell phone has completely lost its charge, so I give up on that pretty quickly. The wallet contains about 20 dollars in cash and a few assorted credit cards. Despite all efforts to shake the contents of the wallet free, there are no revealing slips of paper. The checkbook entries don't contain any secrets either; just a list of paid bills, birthday and holiday gifts to family members. And then I spot a partially made out check, not yet torn out of the book. It has yesterday's date, no name, and is made out in the amount of... Is this possible? I can't believe my eyes, 150,000 dollars. There is a note on the memo line of the check, *Three Paintings.*

First of all, Grandpa can't possibly have that much money. He lives on social security and a small pension from his job with the airline. I remember when I found out that he worked for an airline. I had this image of him in his pilot's uniform, traveling around the world from one exotic location to another. Then I discovered he was an accountant and never left the ground. That was quite a letdown, but I eventually got over it.

One hundred and fifty thousand dollars! No way. And what paintings? I resist the rubber-banded pack of envelopes as long as I can. The envelopes are all sealed. The ink is faded on many of them. The ones that are legible all come from N. Bauer in Amsterdam; not the Amsterdam in the Netherlands, but the one in upstate New York. They are all addressed the same way, to a location Grandpa hasn't lived in for five decades, a place he called *the old neighborhood.*

The letters are all postmarked between 1955 and 1962. Grandpa was born in 1930. He's the accountant, but even I can do this math. If John Robert Orphan and John Robert Bauer are, in fact, the same person, these letters were sent to him when he was somewhere between 25 and 32 years old. That would have been before he married Grandma and certainly before my mother was born. I don't know what to think anymore. I guess it's possible, but none of this makes any sense. And what about the money and the paintings?

My investigation rapidly comes to a stop with the incoming call from Zach.

"Why haven't you answered any of my texts, Robbie? I've been trying to reach you for the last half hour. Your dad is looking for you. Seems you haven't answered his texts either. I covered for you as best I could. Thanks for alerting me to the rehearsal we're having for tomorrow's presentation in Cooper's class. You better get yourself home ASAP because I told your dad you were on the way back."

"Thanks, Zach. It's a long story. I know I owe you an explanation, but just hang in there with me for now."

"Just be grateful that I got to the phone before my mom. Not that it stopped her from checking the caller ID and asking a few hundred questions about why your dad was calling. I put her off for now, but it's only a matter of time before she picks up your scent, Robbie. You'd better get your butt home!"

"I'm on my way."

"From where? Where are you anyway?"

"Not now, Zach. I promise. I'll fill you in tomorrow."

"Should I be worried about you?"

"No, I'm fine. I swear! I'm fine. Just let me get going before my dad gets all worked up and starts asking questions too."

I put the rubber band around the letters and shove everything except Grandpa's cell phone back into the plastic bag. I have no time to look for a particularly good hiding place. Under the bed seems as reasonable a spot as any. I shine the light from my phone to find a clearing amid Grandpa's shoes and his very own collection of dust bunnies.

That is when I see the two brown paper wrapped squares, with a third uncovered one on top. This is no coincidence. They're small, no more than a foot on each side, but there is no question that these are three canvasses…three paintings.

There is not much more investigating I can do now. I have to get out of here. Dad is going to come looking for me any minute. And now I've managed to get Zach in the middle of this. My head feels like it is about to explode. One step at a time. Get everything back under the bed. Make my way down the hallway back to the kitchen, out the back door. Place the key under the doormat. Jump on my bike and stay focused on getting home.

I pedal as fast as I can, just barely catching the traffic light and making the turn back onto Vanderbilt. No chance of slipping back into the house unnoticed. Dad is standing on the lawn, not looking too pleased to see me.

"Robbie, you've been gone for almost two hours. And I'm not at all convinced that you spent all that time at Zach's. In fact, I'm not too sure you were at Zach's at all. What is going on?"

I give serious consideration to lie number six, but nothing. I am out of fuel. Dumb as it may seem, I actually go with the truth—well, mostly.

"I never went to Zach's house, Dad. I was on my way to Zach's but wound up at Grandpa's. I don't know where he was going to or coming from when he had the stroke, but I thought I might be able to figure something out from looking around his house."

"I get it, Robbie. I know how close the two of you are and how upset you are about this. But there is no great mystery here. And if you just would have told me, I might have been able to clear a lot of this up for you."

"I don't get it, Dad. What do you mean, clear this up for me?"

"What did you find in the plastic bag with Grandpa's things, Robbie?"

"Nothing, the bag is in Mom's car!"

"No, it's not, Robbie, and you know it. It was in the laundry room and now it's not. So I'm guessing you grabbed it on your way out to keep it away from your brother."

The only thing worse than lying is being bad at it, and apparently, I really suck at it. Okay, time to regroup and see what Dad actually does know.

"I did take the plastic bag over to Grandpa's. I never intended to open it. I just wanted to keep it safe, and yes, by safe I mean out of Henry's hands."

"But you did—I mean open it, didn't you Robbie?" Dad asks.

Now I am speechless and nodding my head in response to Dad's yes/no questions.

"Did you find Grandpa's checkbook?"

I glance up at Dad, confirming what he already seems to know.

"Did you see a check made out for some paintings?" Dad continues.

I nod again.

"So now you know about the paintings," Dad concludes.

No reply needed at this point. Dad's clearly figured this out already.

"Those paintings were stolen from Grandpa's family in Holland in 1939, just before the outbreak of the war. He's been trying to reclaim them for years."

I hear Dad's words. I just don't know what they mean. "If the paintings were stolen, why is Grandpa paying to get them back?" I ask.

"That's a good question. I just can't seem to get a straight answer from Grandpa," Dad replies. "The only thing he's told me is that without sufficient proof of the origin of the paintings, he has no choice but to buy them back."

"Why are the paintings so important to him?"

"I know Grandpa's told you he was born and raised in Brooklyn. Truth is, he was born in Holland. He was sent to England along with hundreds of other children to escape the German occupation. The rest of his family was deported to concentration camps. He never saw his parents again after that. For Grandpa, the paintings are the only link to his past. Judging from the look on your face, I'm guessing Grandpa never told you that story, Robbie."

"He didn't," I mumble.

"It was just much too painful for him to be reminded of that time in his life," Dad tries to explain.

The power of speech is returning as my mouth begins to form the next set of words. My head is spinning from Dad's revelation. I have so many questions.

"How did the paintings turn up all of a sudden?" I ask.

"I don't know if they have turned up, Robbie. My guess is Grandpa was trying to track them down when he had the stroke. With Grandpa unable to tell us much more, if there were actually any paintings that belonged to his family, they may never be found."

Chapter Eight
Sherlock Holmes

Full disclosure. Dad tells me everything he knows about Grandpa and the paintings. I must admit, it is pretty amazing stuff. It may even help explain Rebecca Bauer's appearance.

I'm done lying for now, but plead guilty to the sin of omission. I am not sure why, but I am just not ready to reveal the location of the paintings, not at least until I have a chance to either get back to the pack of sealed letters addressed to J. R. Bauer or find out exactly what Rebecca knows about Grandpa.

I am up most of the night, trying to piece this whole thing together. With all Grandpa told me over the years, this is one huge story he never mentioned. Dad's explanation makes sense. I get how painful that period of Grandpa's life must be for him. Were any of his stories truthful or were they all a cover-up for what he couldn't bring himself to think about?

I have to stay focused, at least until after school today. I climb over the minefield of debris in the bedroom Henry has left in his wake. He has commandeered the bathroom, so I make my way downstairs to pee and brush my teeth.

Mom and Dad are in an intense conversation in the kitchen and it doesn't take a genius to figure out what they are talking about.

"Dad filled me in on what happened last night, Robbie. We always knew that Grandpa's past would come up someday. We just believed that it was up to him to tell you about it whenever he thought it was the right time."

"Does Henry know any of this, Mom?"

"No, Grandpa insisted that he would decide when to tell each of you."

"Well, I guess that's not going to happen any time soon, if it ever happens at all," I reply.

There is that moment when you are just about to take your parents into your confidence. Sure, I could tell them Grandpa was getting ready to tell me the truth about his past just before the stroke, but something stops me. There is more to this than Amsterdam, the German occupation, the loss of his family, and the paintings. There is Rebecca Bauer, and Mom and Dad don't have a clue about her, or what else she may know about Grandpa. And whatever his reason, Grandpa wants to keep it that way.

"Would you like Henry to drive you to school today, Robbie? I thought it would be nice for you to have some private time together," Mom offers hopefully.

I try to handle this as tactfully as possible, in spite of the severe delusional state my mother is in about my brother and me.

"Mom, Henry just got up. He's in the bathroom and I really don't want to disturb him. I'll meet up with him later. Maybe he can pick me up at the library after school today so you don't have to leave Grandpa alone at the hospital to come get me."

"That's a great idea. Get yourself some breakfast," Dad interrupted. "I'll drop you off at school, and then take Mom to the hospital on my way to the office."

"Sounds like a plan, Dad."

I am temporarily relieved at not having to deal with my brother right now. More importantly, he is likely to be at least an hour late picking me up from the library, which gives me some breathing room to meet up with Sherlock Holmes and the letter that Rebecca promised to leave for me.

Zach rushes over to the car as we pull up to the school building. Dad pops the trunk and we take the science project out. I exhaust every possible hand and eye signal to make sure he doesn't say anything about last night. So far, so good, but I know his silence can't last.

"Are you going to tell me what is going on?" Zach loud whispers between his clenched teeth as we walk up the stairs.

"Can we just stay focused on the science presentation? I'm trying to concentrate on the symbiotic relationship between nitrogen, plants, and bacteria," I answer. I don't really want to go into this any further, at least not now.

"How about taking a few minutes to concentrate on the trouble you almost got us both into last night?" Zach persists.

"Look, there are some very strange things going on with my grandfather, and it's even more complicated with him not being able to speak because of the stroke." I do everything I can to change the topic. But Zach is not letting me off the hook.

Thankfully, Mr. Cooper appears on the stairwell and escorts us to the gym where the other science projects are already on display.

"This doesn't end here, Robbie. I want details after school today," Zach insists.

As if I don't have enough to worry about. Now I have to deal with Zach on top of everything else. If past experience predicts the future, he will hound me until I let him in on this.

"Can you come up with some excuse to hang out with me at the library after school today?" I ask. "Just tell your mom Henry is picking us up and will drop you off at home."

"Are you seriously asking me to get into the car with that brother of yours, Robbie?"

"That depends on just how much you want to know what's going on with me," I reply.

"Oh, the sacrifices one makes for friendship," Zach responds sarcastically.

"Yes, or curiosity killed the cat. Have your pick," I answer.

The science project is a hit. Cooper thinks we might have a shot at winning the science fair. The day seems to drag on endlessly. Dismissal is at 2:55, and Zach is right on schedule, waiting in front of my homeroom.

The questioning begins as soon as we are out of the building. I give Zach the brief rundown, the basics about Grandpa's stroke, his childhood escape from Holland, the unopened letters, and Rebecca Bauer.

"What's in the library?" Zach asks.

"Sherlock Holmes."

"Look, I know you have some kind of strange family mystery going on here, Robbie, but Sherlock Holmes, really? You know he's just a fictional character?"

"Yes, I know he's a fictional character, but that's what I'm supposed to look for—the book, not the person, Zach. Rebecca Bauer, who claims that her grandfather and mine were brothers, is supposed to leave some sort of letter stuck between the pages of the book for me to read."

If Zach asks me one more question, I think I will lose it. Why did I involve him in this, anyway? Well, what's done is done. Next steps—the librarian, Sherlock Holmes, the letter.

I charge up the steps of the library with Zach on my heels and make my way to the front desk.

"You know, that's an interesting coincidence, young man. You're the third person who asked for *The Complete Collection of Sherlock Holmes* today," the librarian explains.

"The third person?"

"Yes, a charming young girl, not much older than you, came in during lunchtime and requested the book. And about an hour later, an elderly woman in a wheelchair came in and asked for the same book. I definitely remember her because she didn't speak English very well, and her aide did most of the talking. I'm afraid the book is not available because the woman borrowed it. I have other Sherlock Holmes volumes, but not the complete collection. It's not due back for two weeks."

Chapter Nine
So It Is Written

Deserted by Sherlock Holmes and not a clue about what to do next. At least Sherlock had Dr. Watson. Who am I left with? Zach! As if that is not bad enough, for the first time in his life, Henry arrives on time to pick us up from the library. I read the incoming text. *Waiting out front for u. Move it bro.*

There is not much more I can do here anyway. At least I can free myself from Zach for a while and visit Grandpa at the hospital. I have to let Rebecca know I never got the letter. Is it just a coincidence that some old lady took the book out of the library, or does she figure into this somehow too?

"I can call my mom and tell her I'm going to the hospital with you to see your grandfather," Zach declares.

"Not a good idea. He's in ICU and visitors are strictly limited to immediate family."

"If I didn't know better, I'd think you're trying to get rid of me."

"Of course not," I answer unconvincingly. "I just need some time to think. I promise I'll call you later."

We drop Zach off. Now I have to deal with Henry.

"What are you and your dorky buddy up to?" Henry asks in his typically insulting way.

"Nothing that would interest you. Just take me to the hospital to see Grandpa."

The next 15 minutes pass in complete silence except for the beeping sound from Henry's phone, signaling one text after another.

"You can do whatever you want when I'm not in the car. Just don't answer those while I'm sitting in the death seat," I plead with Henry. "I'd like to walk into the hospital on my two feet, not be carried in through the emergency room."

"Very funny. Don't worry, I'll get you there, but not before you tell me what's going on."

I consider what else I might reveal to Henry without going into too much detail. Fortunately, my temporary insanity is interrupted by Mom's call. She tells me that the speech therapist visited Grandpa several times today. Even though he is not yet saying anything that anyone can understand, he can use his left hand to write.

"That's great, Mom. Henry and I are almost there. We'll meet you up at ICU in a few minutes," I respond, hoping that will put a stop to Henry's questions.

"You're off the hook, for now, Robbie, but we're not done with this conversation."

Well, we're done for now and that is all that matters. There are two things I have to focus on. I need to contact Rebecca about the letter and see if there is any more information I can get from Grandpa.

Mom is outside the ICU when Henry and I get out of the elevator. The doctors are checking on Grandpa so the wait continues. I settle into a seat as far away from my brother as possible. He is in full throttle texting mode and thankfully distracted. Mom is chatting with some lady who is there to see a patient.

The doctors emerge. The news is good. Grandpa is stable and moving to another floor. We can stay with him until he goes to the new room. There is no way I'm going to get any time alone with him. I just need to stay away from Henry for now. With any luck, he will get bored pretty quickly and make his exit before long.

That is when the flowers arrive. The nurse steps into the room to show us a beautiful bouquet of lilies that was just delivered for Grandpa. Hospital policy does not permit flowers in the ICU, so she will have them brought to Grandpa's new room. She just wants to make sure we see them first.

"Oh, that's so lovely," Mom exclaims. "Who are they from? There must be a card."

The nurse removes the small envelope clipped to the cellophane wrapping and hands it to Mom. She opens it and seems puzzled as she reads aloud.

The flowers speak for themselves, and perhaps for you too. Wishing you well!

"That's strange. There's no name. Dad, does this make any sense to you?" Mom asks Grandpa, looking for an explanation.

It must, because in his now clearly recognizable way, Grandpa nods his head in an unmistakably affirmative reply. Mom follows the nurse and the flowers out of the room. She is no less curious than she was a moment ago, but the move is about to begin as nurses disconnect the wires and tubes, and orderlies appear at Grandpa's door to transport his bed to the neurology unit.

We are asked to go to the sixth-floor waiting room until the transfer is complete. Henry doesn't seem to notice the flowers, and as predicted, his patience for hospitals wears thin.

"Mom, I'm going to head out. Grandpa, I'll see you tomorrow," he announces. Me, I just get the death stare.

"It's going to take a while until they get Grandpa set up in the new room. Let me walk you to the parking lot, sweetie. You must be exhausted."

Mom actually says that to Henry. "You must be exhausted." Is she kidding? She has hardly slept in three days. That is about all that Henry has done, other than driving back and forth to the hospital a few times, texting his friends, and busting my chops. This *Henry the Hero* thing is something else.

The truth is I am relieved to have Henry out of my way for now. Maybe I can track Rebecca down in these few minutes I have alone. I reach for my phone when one of the nurses tries to get my attention.

"I think this belongs to your grandfather. It must have fallen off the bed when they moved him," the nurse explains as she hands me a small notepad. "The speech therapist was getting him to write down some words so that he would be less frustrated about speaking."

I thank her and glance at the notepad. Grandpa is a righty. He must have written these words with his left hand because the printing is kind of shaky. I recognize my name,

Robbie, my brother's, *Henry*, Mom's name, *Emily*, and Dad's name, *Ben*. The therapist probably asked him to name the people in the family. There is another name on the next page, *Bauer*, and another word, *poppenhuis*, which makes no sense to me.

I doubt that the notepad fell off Grandpa's bed accidentally. He must have dropped it deliberately, hoping it would find its way to me. He must be signaling some kind of connection to the name Bauer. That has to be what he was going to tell me before the stroke.

My phone vibrates with an incoming text from Mom. *Meet me in the sixth-floor waiting area.* I stuff the notepad into my pocket and head for the elevator. The door opens, revealing a crowd of visitors making their way to patients' rooms. I am about to step in when someone grabs me by the arm.

Chapter Ten
Truth Be Told

Okay, I know I'm a little jumpy given the events of the last two days, but when some stranger grabs your arm out of nowhere, it's pretty darn freaky.

"I didn't mean to startle you. I just need a few moments of your time," the man says in a distinctly accented voice.

I find myself facing a well-dressed bearded middle-aged man who apologizes as he releases my arm. He summons me to the waiting area, promising to detain me only briefly. I don't know why, but for some strange reason, I do as he asks.

"I am an acquaintance of Mrs. Lillian Bauer," the man begins to explain. "I believe you are familiar with Mrs. Bauer."

"I'm more familiar with the name Bauer than I'd like to be, but I have no idea who Mrs. Lillian Bauer is," I reply anxiously. I know I need to get to the sixth floor before my mother sends out the National Guard.

"Yes, I realize that. But I believe you have made the acquaintance of her granddaughter, Rebecca," he continues.

"Well, I wouldn't exactly say that either. I've had some bizarre phone calls from her, but that's about it. Look, I don't know what you have to do with this whole Bauer family affair, but I need to get to my grandfather's room."

"I understand, and I believe I can clear some of this up for you," he declares.

"Sure, and I guess you are, let me see…another long lost relative of mine."

"Well, in fact, I am not a relative of yours, and neither is Rebecca Bauer," he says quite emphatically. "Rebecca is a young lady with a very active imagination. I'm afraid she has concocted a tale of family intrigue which bears little resemblance to the truth."

The man finally introduces himself as Josef DeKlerk, an art dealer from the Netherlands. He informs me that he is the one who met with Grandpa the other night, just before he had the stroke. Mr. DeKlerk explains that he recently acquired a number of paintings that were recovered from various art galleries in Europe. Several of the paintings led him to Mrs. Lillian Bauer, who then put him in touch with Grandpa.

Considering what Dad told me yesterday, about stolen paintings and everything, I guess that makes sense. But what does this DeKlerk guy want with me, anyway?

"So then what's the connection between the Bauer family and my grandfather?" I ask, not knowing what to believe at this point.

"I'm not entirely certain. I believe that your grandfather and Lillian Bauer's deceased husband, Nathan Bauer, were childhood friends in Amsterdam. I know that Rebecca is convinced that they were not merely friends, but were, in fact, brothers. However, her grandmother, Lillian, vehemently denies that. She attributes the notion of a blood relationship to a completely unfounded fantasy invented by Rebecca," Mr. DeKlerk attempts to clarify.

"Okay, so how do I figure into all of this? What do you want from me?" I ask.

"Actually, I don't want anything. My task is only to conclude the business of returning the paintings to their rightful owners and to collect a small commission for my efforts. Had your grandfather not been taken ill, this whole matter would have been resolved by now," DeKlerk tries to explain.

"But he is ill and can't clear any of this up at the moment."

"I'm aware of that, and so is Mrs. Bauer. She simply asks that you ignore all further attempts that her granddaughter makes to contact you."

I don't get it. What possible reason would Rebecca have for making up this story about the Bauer brothers? I still have no clue what was in the letter Rebecca tried to leave at the library for me, or even if there was a letter. Letter or not, there must have been something I wasn't supposed to see. Someone went to the trouble to get hold of *The Complete Collection of Sherlock Holmes* before I could. And I don't think it's too much of a stretch to figure that the old woman who got to the book first was Mrs. Lillian Bauer, Rebecca's grandmother.

My cell phone signals an incoming text—not at all unexpected—from Mom. *Where r u? R you ok?* My brain is on overload. I've got a million thoughts crashing into each other, and the one person who might be able to make any sense out of this can't do much more than scribble a name on a notepad.

"I've got to get downstairs, Mr. DeKlerk. You want me to stay clear of Rebecca. Okay, I will!"

"When do you think I might be able to speak with your grandfather again?" DeKlerk inquires.

"No time soon, as far as I can tell. First of all, there is no way the doctors and especially my mother, are going to let anyone outside of the family anywhere near him. And even if you could see him, there's not much he would be able to tell you. The stroke has pretty much taken care of that."

I am about to ask DeKlerk about the paintings I found in Grandpa's room and stop myself mid-sentence. If DeKlerk was trying to return or sell paintings to Grandpa, then where did the three paintings come from that I found under the bed? And why did Grandpa have a check made out for 150,000 dollars for paintings he already had?

DeKlerk trails after me as I rush to get into the elevator before the doors close. "Take my card, young man. Call me as soon as your grandfather can have visitors. And please respect Mrs. Bauer's wishes. Do not contact Rebecca," he insists.

I guess DeKlerk is not up on his child psychology. He may know about art, but he sure doesn't know much about kids, especially this kid. The last thing you do if you want a kid not to do something is tell him not to do it. I don't know how or when but I just know I have to find Rebecca. Maybe we're related, maybe not. But there is more to this story than the return of stolen paintings.

Chapter Eleven
Nothing Is as It Seems

I've learned one thing in the last few days. Nobody really knows the truth. And if someone does, there is a good chance they will do whatever it takes to keep you from finding it out. Oh sure, they will make you think they are letting you in on something that no one else knows, but don't believe it for a minute. If you want to know what's real, you better not take anyone else's word for it. It is very clear now. If I'm ever going to get to the bottom of this, I'll have to do it on my own.

That basically means one thing. I have to get back to Grandpa's house to check out the packet of unopened letters and the paintings under the bed. But I can't do that just yet. Mom is waiting for me on the sixth floor. Grandpa must be settled in his room by now, and I better do some fast-talking to explain to Mom why I've been missing in action all this time.

The elevator opens on the sixth floor directly opposite the nurse's station. It seems Mom is occupied at the moment, so I'm in the clear for now. She is standing outside of what I'm guessing is Grandpa's room talking to a nurse. She spots me and motions for me to come over.

"Anna, this is my son, Robbie. Robbie, this is Anna, Grandpa's nurse," Mom announces.

"So you're the young man your grandfather has been trying to tell me about. He's been very anxious to see you, Robbie," the nurse declares. "Just give me a few more minutes to finish setting things up, and you can spend some time with him. Why don't you get a snack or something in the cafeteria? I should be done in about 20 minutes. Oh, and by the way, if he has a cell phone, you can leave it for him now that he's out of ICU."

"I think we left it at home with his other things," Mom explains to the nurse.

"Actually, I have it, Mom," I admit, pulling it from my backpack. Mom seems puzzled but doesn't question me further. "It needs to be charged," I say as I hand it to Anna.

"No worries, I'll take care of it and leave it in his bedside drawer," Anna replies.

Mom puts her arm around me and we head back to the elevator. She is not happy about leaving Grandpa and has no interest in eating but agrees to take the break.

"When the nurse said that Grandpa was trying to tell her about me, did she mean he was actually talking?" I ask hopefully.

"Not really, Robbie. It's pretty much the same gibberish and occasionally a recognizable syllable. But he's figured out how to flirt with the nurses, so I guess that's a good sign."

"What about writing?" I ask.

"I guess he was doing some of that with the speech therapist. Come to think of it, I don't know what happened to the notebook she was using with him."

"Oh, that. The ICU nurse found it and gave it to me after they took Grandpa down to his room."

"Did Grandpa write anything in it?" Mom asks.

Now, what do I say? I guess there is no harm in telling her the truth, well at least partly. "The only thing he wrote in it was our names."

I don't mention anything about the name *Bauer*, or that other word. Not yet. I have to figure things out for myself first. Mom may know about Grandpa's childhood and the art that was stolen from his family, but I'm pretty sure she has no idea he may have a long lost brother. The operative word being *may*, since according to DeKlerk, no matter what Rebecca thinks, he doesn't.

The elevator stops on just about every floor on our way down to the hospital lobby. Random visitors, white-coated doctors, nurses, and lab technicians stare intently at the display of floor numbers as they light up one after the other. A few people are chatting, but even they don't look at each other. Everyone wants out, and the more crowded it gets, the more trouble I have breathing.

The rest is a blur. I guess if you're going to pass out, a hospital is a pretty good place to do it. I'm not sure how long I was out, but the next thing I know, I smell this awful stuff and I can't stop coughing.

Two security guards help me to my feet and position me on a nearby bench. "Are you okay, young man?"

"I guess so," I answer. "What happened?"

"Seems like it got little claustrophobic in there for you, kid."

"Where's my mom?"

"Don't worry. She didn't go too far. The docs want to check you out. She's filling out some paperwork. We're gonna put you in this wheelchair and meet her over at the ER."

This is all pretty weird, but I'm not about to argue with these guys. My head is throbbing, and I'm feeling pretty woozy. I better get this checked out. Mom certainly doesn't need another patient to worry about.

The taller of the two security guys gets me settled in the wheelchair and starts off toward the ER. I get a couple of nods and smiles from people who must have heard about the kid who fainted in the elevator.

Mom approaches with a distinctly worried look on her face. She is pale. Her hair, which never has a single strand out of place, is frazzled and pointing in several different directions.

"Robbie, you gave me quite a scare back there. One minute you were standing next to me. The next you hit the ground."

"I don't know Mom. The only thing I remember was that it was kind of stuffy in there. The rest is a blank."

"They want to do some routine tests just to make sure you're okay. I'm going to go back up to Grandpa for a few minutes. The ER nurse will look after you. Dad is on his way and should be here any minute," Mom explains.

My head starts to clear and I realize I don't have my backpack or my phone. "Mom, where's my stuff?"

"I don't know, Robbie. I handed it to some man who helped me get you out of the elevator. He waited with me until the security guards came and then he disappeared."

"Oh, don't worry, young man. We have your backpack. The gentleman left it with us on his way out. It's in the office," the guard interrupted.

The next thing I know, I am whisked away by a nurse who introduces himself as Carlos. I get poked and prodded for about three hours. Mom and Dad take turns checking on me between tests. I get the thumbs up. All is well. Backpack returned. No diagnosis. No phone!

It turns out the backpack was returned by the kind gentleman who helped take me out of the elevator. The only problem is that the well-dressed bearded man with a distinctly accented voice, as my mother later described him, left with my phone and the only way I had of contacting Rebecca.

Chapter Twelve
The Shortest Distance Between
Two Points

It doesn't take a rocket scientist to figure out who has my phone. But the missing phone may be just the break I need to locate Rebecca. Not that Mom and Dad ever used it to spy on me. But when I turned 12 and got my own phone, it was on condition that they install a GPS tracking app.

Sure, I have DeKlerk's business card and could just call him. But why give him a heads up. If I can track the phone, I can find DeKlerk. If I can find DeKlerk, that might just put me one step closer to Rebecca, the letter, and the truth about Grandpa.

I exit the ER, flanked by my security detail, Mom and Dad. It is clear that I am not getting back upstairs to see Grandpa. Doctors' orders are that I go home and take it easy. While the test results are all normal, everyone has concluded that the emotional upset of Grandpa's stroke has gotten to me and that I need a break from the hospital.

"Don't argue with us, Robbie. Dad is going to take you home and get you some dinner. If you're feeling okay, you can visit with Grandpa tomorrow after school," Mom insists.

The truth is that as much as I would love to check in with Grandpa again, I need to get away from this place for a while. I mount a bit of a protest, just to keep it real, but surrender to my parents' will with just the right amount of credibility.

The real problem is that I need to track my phone without letting on that it's missing, and that means without asking my parents if I can use either of their phones. That leaves only one other option, and it's one I know I am going to regret—Zach.

There is no choice. Zach and I shared our tracking information when we got our phones last year. As much as I know this is going to complicate things, it sure beats trying to explain any of this to Mom and Dad.

"Let's get you home, Robbie. Do you have all of your things?" Dad asks.

"I think so," I answer, a bit dazed. I am definitely preoccupied with trying to figure out how to get in touch with Zach.

Dad places his arm around my shoulder and escorts me out of the hospital. There is just enough of a chill in the air to shake me out of my stupor. I sit up front as we head out of the parking lot toward home.

"How about we stop for some take-out, Robbie?" Dad asks.

"Sure Dad, whatever you want."

"Are you okay with Chinese, Robbie?"

"Sure Dad, whatever."

Dad places the call to Shanghai Palace. It's the restaurant we always go to with Grandpa, just about ten minutes from his house. It takes us about 20 minutes to get there. With any luck, Dad will leave his phone in the car when he goes in to pick up the food. That will give me the chance to track my phone without having to involve Zach for the moment.

Dad turns off the engine, takes the key out of the ignition, reaches for his wallet, and unlocks the door. Just as he is about to walk out of the car and leave the phone on the center console, it rings. Give me a break, he is actually just about to walk out of the car without the phone and it rings.

Dad checks the caller ID. It's Henry.

"Robbie, please get it and see what your brother wants. I'll be right back."

Henry is not the person I particularly want to talk to, but if that's what it takes to be alone with Dad's phone, I'll deal with my big brother.

"What's up?" I ask, as politely as possible under the circumstances.

"Where's Dad? I need to talk to him."

"We stopped off to pick up some take-out. What's the emergency?"

"Get him for me now, Robbie. I need to talk to him," Henry demands.

Under normal conditions, I would take full advantage of the rare opportunity to have the upper hand on Henry. Truth is though, he sounds pretty desperate. And there is not much that is normal about anything that has happened in the last couple of days.

"Dad's on his way back to the car. Hang on a second."

I stick my hand out of the open window and hand the phone to Dad. "It's Henry and he doesn't sound too good," I explain.

All I hear on my end is, "Yes. Okay. Are you alright? Where are you? Oh for heaven's sake, Henry. Not again."

Dad ends the call and looks pretty grim as he gets back into the driver's seat. "Robbie, I'm going to drop you off at home. I have to pick up your brother. Can you manage by yourself for a little while? I'll get back as soon as I can."

"What happened, Dad?"

"You've got enough on your mind right now. Let me just handle this with your brother before Mom gets home."

I have no clue what's going on with Henry. And it doesn't look like I'm going to get any more information from Dad, at least not now. Henry has clearly gotten himself into some sort of mess. No surprise there. Dad is going to do whatever it takes to rescue him, and more importantly, he is going to keep Mom out of it at all costs.

There is something strangely familiar about all of this. I know it seems a little heartless, but I just can't worry about Henry. If past experience has taught me anything, it is to get out of the way of my big brother's chaos. I can't say I'm not curious, but I really have other things to attend to at the moment.

Dad drops me off at the house. He takes his phone with him, which means I'm back to Plan Zach. I unlock the door, deposit my backpack on the kitchen counter, and grab the house phone. I just hope that Zach is home and that I can get what I need from him without a million questions.

Thankfully Zach answers the phone and I don't have to make polite small talk with his mom. "I've been calling you for hours. Where have you been?" Zach asks.

"I don't have my phone," I explain.

"Why not?"

"Because I lost it. And don't ask me how. I just did. And I need you to do something for me," I continue.

"At your service."

"You know that tracking app we both installed on our phones. Check to see if you can locate my phone."

"Easy, peasy. Hold on a second. Got it right here!"

"Well, can you tell where it is?"

"Were you back at your grandfather's house?" Zach asks.

"Why?"

"Because that's where you must have left your phone," Zach answers. "Dorchester and Vanderbilt, 699 Dorchester to be exact. That's your grandfather's address, isn't it?"

Every bone in my body tells me I'm going to regret my next sentence, but it doesn't seem as if I have much of a choice.

"Zach, I need your help."

Chapter Thirteen
Lost and Found

The good news is that Zach lives only three blocks from Grandpa's house. The bad news is that I don't have a clue about what to tell him to do, even if he can get over there. And that is a pretty big if, considering it is after 9 pm on a school night.

"Robbie, you better come clean. What is going on with your phone? If you didn't leave it at your grandfather's house, how did it get there?"

"It went missing at the hospital."

"Okay, keep going. Now I know where you lost it. How did it make its way across town to your grandfather's house?"

I realize there is no point in holding out any longer and give Zach the condensed version of the past few days. For once, he is unusually quiet and hardly asks any questions.

"Are you there, Zach? How come you're not saying anything?"

"You fainted and this DeKlerk guy made off with your phone?" Zach finally asks.

"And that means I have no way of contacting Rebecca and getting to the bottom of this," I try to explain.

"I have about a million more questions, but I also think I have a plan," Zach interrupts.

And he does. Zach actually has an idea. I don't know how good it is and if it will work, but I don't have many options at this point.

"Let's call your grandfather's phone, his house phone. DeKlerk won't answer it, of course. But he will hear the message we leave on the answering machine."

"And exactly what message am I leaving?"

"Not you. Me!" Zach insists.

"What do you mean, you?" I ask, not having a clue where Zach is headed.

"I mean I get DeKlerk to think you're on the way over to your grandfather's house. I get really dramatic. I say I'm not sure you're there yet, call me as soon as you get this message, and be careful!"

Zach concocts this pretty cool plan to get DeKlerk to expect me at Grandpa's house within minutes. If he buys it and takes off, we can use my phone to track him back to the Bauer residence, and possibly Rebecca, we hope.

But what if he doesn't buy it? What if he waits for me to get there so that he can confront me again? And what is he doing at Grandpa's, anyway? Whatever DeKlerk and Grandpa met about before the stroke set something in motion, but what?

"Robbie, are we doing this or not?" Zach interjects anxiously.

"Sure. Make the call," I agree reluctantly.

I listen as Zach puts his house phone on speaker and makes the call from his cell on the other end. The phone rings four times, goes to voicemail, and I hold my breath.

Zach goes into full Shakespeare mode when someone answers the phone.

I pray that Zach doesn't say a word and just gets off the phone. Needless to say, that is one prayer that doesn't get answered.

"Who is this?" Zach asks.

The question is expected. The answer is not.

"Is that you, Robbie? It's Rebecca."

"It's not Robbie. It's Zach!"

"Who?"

"Zach, Robbie's friend, and I'm looking for Robbie."

"Give it a break, Zach. Your acting career is over," I shout, hoping Rebecca realizes it's me.

"What are you guys up to, and where are you?" Rebecca asks.

"Where are we? What are you doing at Mr. Orphan's house?" Zach demands.

As this ridiculous three-way interrogation continues, I hear my dad's car pull into the driveway. The driver and passenger doors slam shut in rapid sequence. That no doubt means I will soon have the pleasure of my big brother's company again. There is only one thing left for me to do, hang up before this gets even more complicated. Where does that leave Rebecca, Grandpa, DeKlerk, and the stolen art? In Zach's hands. What could possibly go wrong? Everything!

Chapter Fourteen
Between a Rock and a Hard Place

Dad asks me if there is any Chinese food left over. Henry doesn't say a word. Despite his best efforts to conceal his face, an angry swollen eye is barely visible under his sweatshirt hood. He avoids making eye contact and hurries past me up the stairs to our room.

"What happened, Dad?"

"I don't think your brother wants me going into it."

"Is he okay?" I ask. My brother is no stranger to trouble, but this seems different.

"He'll be fine. It's nothing you have to worry about," Dad reassures me.

"Well, you look pretty worried, Dad."

"I'm not sure it's worry or exhaustion, or just figuring out how to keep this from your mother. It's been one thing after another and this is the last thing she needs on her head right now."

Dad switches the subject back to me. I make up some excuse for why I haven't eaten and some explanation for what I've been up to since he left me at home and raced off to get Henry.

Both the house phone and Dad's cell ring simultaneously. Dad reaches for the cell and asks me to pick up the house phone. He has Mom on the line and predictably the caller ID on the house phone signals that it is Zach. Dad steps away to speak with Mom, which gives me the momentary privacy I need.

"How did Rebecca get hold of my phone and what is she doing at my grandfather's house?" I blurt into the phone, trying to keep my voice out of Dad's earshot.

"I don't know," Zach answers.

"Well, what did she tell you?"

"She didn't tell me anything. But I know she wasn't at the house alone because she hung up the phone when some guy walked in and called her name."

"It had to be DeKlerk. Did he have an accent?"

"I couldn't really tell. All he said was her name."

"I just want to know how they got in and what they were doing there. Is there anything else you can think of, Zach?"

"Nothing else except your battery must have finally gone dead because I'm not getting a signal anymore."

Now I have no phone, no way of contacting Rebecca, and no clue as to how or why she and DeKlerk were, or still are, in my grandfather's house. Zach is yammering away on the other end, half talking to me and half trying to convince his mother that we'll be off the phone in a minute.

"Robbie, I have to get off the phone. Just tell me how DeKlerk figured out where your grandfather lives," Zach insists.

"His address and phone number are in my contacts."

"DeKlerk couldn't have gotten into your phone anyway without your passcode," Zach reminds me. "Please don't tell me you still use 1-2-3-4 as your passcode."

"Well, I've been meaning to change it. I just never got around to it," I hesitate, now realizing I have made it completely possible for DeKlerk to access anything he might need from my phone.

"You never changed the passcode?" Zach asks incredulously. "Are you kidding me? What else is on the phone?" Zach asks.

And then I remember. Just before I shoved the three paintings back under the bed in Grandpa's bedroom, I took a photo of the one that was partially unwrapped. DeKlerk insisted that he was trying to return stolen art to my grandfather. I don't buy that anymore. There is something in that house that DeKlerk is after.

"Robbie, are you still there?"

"Zach, we have to get over to my grandfather's house ASAP."

"Robbie, it's almost 10 pm. How do you propose we do that?"

Dad walks into the room to tell me that Mom is on her way home. There is no change in Grandpa's condition, but he is resting comfortably. Dad offers me another chance to have the now-cold Chinese food. If not, he wants me in my room and in bed before Mom arrives. Most importantly, he asks me to stay clear of Henry for now.

I now truly understand what it means when people say they are stuck between a rock and a hard place. I have no choice but to get off the phone with Zach and let things go, at least until tomorrow.

The house is unusually quiet, particularly with Henry home. The silence is a sharp contrast with the chatter in my head. I realize there is not much I can do until the morning. I resign myself to a sleepless night trying to figure out what to do next. Dad hugs me and points me in the direction of the staircase. He reminds me not to wake Henry. I climb the stairs and open the door of the room just enough to light my way around the cluttered floor to my bed.

"Shut the door. I need to talk to you. Did Dad tell you what happened?" Henry whispers.

"No! But I saw what your eye looks like, so anyone with half a brain can figure you got into some sort of fight."

"It's no big deal. I just don't want Mom to find out with everything else that's going on."

"Seems like we're all on the same page where that's concerned."

What a pleasant surprise to hear Henry actually think about someone else for a change. He doesn't offer much of an explanation but unexpectedly asks for my help. For someone who barely acknowledges my existence, this is indeed a strange request. And what does my big brother want? He wants Mom and Dad to think he is going back to school for a few days while he holes up at Grandpa's.

At first, this seems totally insane, not to mention impossible to pull off. But on second thought, this might just work, and in more ways than one. The plan is simple. Once Mom and Dad are asleep, Henry makes his way downstairs to the garage. He takes my bike. I give him the rundown on how to get into Grandpa's house through the back door. He plans to hang out there for a couple of days but offers no other explanation.

My job is to come up with some reasonable excuse for Henry's sudden return to school, prepare a note on my laptop, and leave it for Mom and Dad to find in the morning. Gratitude from Henry is a bit startling. To say the least, I am not used to it. He must be in an awfully big mess to turn to me like this. And I must be slightly delusional to think that this can end well.

Chapter Fifteen
All Eyes Are on Henry

Despite the odds against sleep, I must have fallen out after I left the note, supposedly from Henry, in the kitchen last night. I think I may have been too convincing. Mom is gushing over her elder son's responsible decision to not miss too many classes. Dad, on the other hand, seems pretty doubtful about Henry's unusual sense of duty. But for the moment, he is not letting on, at least to Mom.

Mom is relieved to know Henry is on his way back to school. Dad is thankful not to deal with Henry for now. I'm just grateful for a reason to get out of the house before either of them senses my imminent nervous breakdown. And then I remember I don't have my bike.

"Dad, can you drop me off at school on your way to work?"

"I figured you would take your bike and meet up with Zach this morning if you're feeling okay. I just moved it out of the garage so I wouldn't hit it when I pull out. And you really need to be more careful about keeping your phone charged. I found it on a shelf next to the bike and plugged it in for you. It should have just enough juice to get you through the day."

Forget the nervous breakdown. Clearly, I am losing my mind. I pick up my backpack, stuff the sandwich Mom made into one of the pockets, and retrieve my phone from Dad's outstretched arm. I reach for the phone as it signals an incoming text.

"It looks like it's from Henry," Dad whispers, cautious not to be overheard by Mom. "What's going on, Robbie?" he continues almost inaudibly. "We both know Henry doesn't have his car to get himself back to school. Where is he?"

Dad follows me out through the side door to the driveway. There, my bike waits without any hint of how it made its way back from Grandpa's house. Any hope of a quick escape is cut short as Dad grasps hold of the handlebars and blocks my path. His questions are predictable. My answers come as a complete surprise, even to me.

"Where is your brother?"

"He's at Grandpa's."

"What's he doing there?"

"Look, I don't know what happened to him. Remember, you decided not to tell me last night. All I know is that he didn't want Mom to see him looking like he ran into a bus. He asked me to help him out. I did. That's all I know!"

Dad seems satisfied that I have no other information to offer. He releases my handlebars and steps away from the bike. I step on the pedal, hoist myself onto the seat, and take off. I barely hear Dad as he asks one last question, "What did Henry text?"

A reasonable question from Dad under the circumstances, just not one I ask myself as I figure out my next move. I am in possession of a bike and phone that inexplicably reappeared at my house sometime last night. The only connection between my bike and phone is my grandfather's house. And who is probably sound asleep at that very location? My useless brother. On second thought, I hit the brakes and pull over. The only thing that makes sense is that, in typical Henry fashion, the message makes no sense. *Package delivered.*

There is no way I am going to school. Thankfully, Zach answers my call.

"How did you get your phone back?" Zach asks, a reasonable question under the circumstances.

"I'm not sure, but I need you to meet me at my grandfather's house."

"You mean after school?"

"No, I mean now!"

"What's going on, Robbie?"

"Henry got into some kind of trouble last night and needed a place to go."

"And you sent him to your grandfather's house with Rebecca and DeKlerk there? Are you nuts?"

"When you put it that way, yes, I guess I am crazy. I was just hoping that with him showing up, if they were still there, they would take off. And if they were gone already, Henry could hold down the fort until we got there today," I explain.

"Are we talking about the same brother? You put him in the middle of anything and there's only one way for things to go—wrong!"

"I know that, but he was desperate, and so was I."

"Give me about 15 minutes. I have to wait until my parents leave so they don't see me take off in the opposite direction from school. I'll be there," Zach reassures me.

No point in waiting for Zach. I am only five minutes away from Grandpa's. The sooner I get there, the better. I think about calling Henry to announce my arrival and decide that is probably not the best idea. Let me just get there and check things out for myself.

The street's usual sleepy tree-lined appearance is altered by the unfamiliar white van that heads away down the block. I jump off the bike and race up the steps to the back porch. The door is unlocked. Henry is asleep on the couch. His black eye has taken on a vivid multi-colored appearance. In fact, his whole face seems disfigured and badly bruised. I try to wake him. Having seen him in a stoned-out stupor many times before, I know he is not dead. He is breathing all right, shallow perhaps, but there is enough rise and fall of his chest for me to know he is alive.

The house seems undisturbed, at least on first inspection. Zach arrives and shakes his head knowingly at the sight of Henry. "What did he get himself into this time?" Zach wonders aloud.

"I don't have a clue, and I have no idea who or what he found when he got here last night."

I head for Grandpa's room with Zach on my heels. I look around, get down on my hands and knees, and move my hand from side to side under the bed. I recover the plastic bag with Grandpa's things and slide down on my back to extend my reach. Nothing! The paintings are gone! In their place, there is a business card belonging to Josef

DeKlerk. On the card, I see one handwritten word, *Provenance*, whatever that means.

"What are you looking for, little bro?" Henry mumbles as he shuffles into the room.

"Was anyone in the house when you got here last night?" I am on my feet in full detective mode, staring at my brother who is barely standing at all.

"You know. There was something weird. You gave me this whole routine to follow to get into the house, but the back door was unlocked when I got here. I pretty much passed out on the couch after that and didn't give it much thought."

"Did you look around or see anything else, Henry? Think—it's important!"

"I had a pretty rough night and was just glad to make it here on that bike of yours."

"Do you remember texting me?"

"I was out of it, but not that out of it. I never texted you, Robbie."

"Where's your phone?" I demand.

"I must have left it in the bathroom with my keys when I emptied my pockets before I fell out," Henry adds, patting himself down just to be certain.

"So the only rooms you were in last night were the bathroom and the living room?"

"I guess so. Why do you care which rooms I was in? What's with all the questions?" Henry asks, becoming increasingly agitated.

There is not much point in keeping Henry in the dark any longer. I have to decide what he absolutely needs to know, and what would just complicate things even more.

Zach slips past me to retrieve Henry's phone from the bathroom. I show Henry the text, which he insists he never sent.

"I'm pretty sure someone was in the house when you got here last night. Whoever was here found what he was looking for and took off with it after you fell asleep," I explain.

"Are you saying the house was robbed while I was sleeping?"

"Yes and no," I reply.

"Which is it, yes or no?" Henry asks.

"Something was taken, but it wasn't exactly a robbery."

While it is usually Henry who talks in circles and makes no sense, I am doing a pretty good job of it myself now. Zach's penetrating stare tells me I better quit while I'm ahead, although I don't really think I am ahead at the moment. It is just that I am not saying anything I will regret, I hope.

"We've got to get to school, Robbie," Zach interrupts.

"Yeah, we've got to get out of here. Will you be okay, Henry? You better pay some attention to that eye."

"Not so fast, little bro. I want you back here after school today or I call in Mom and Dad, and you get to be the one with more explaining to do than me for a change."

Zach makes his way to the front door as I assure my brother I will return after school. In the several seconds it takes me to catch up with Zach, he does an about-face and slams the door shut behind him. He points in the direction of the driveway, now occupied by the white van whose exit from the street earlier seemed so unusual. More surprising is the passenger, make that passengers, who emerge from the vehicle.

Chapter Sixteen
One Word Leads to Another

One handwritten word on DeKlerk's business card, *Provenance*. Talk about going in circles. The word *provenance* comes from the French word *provenir*, which means *to come from*. I google it and learn it has something to do with the chronology of ownership, custody, or location of a historical object, usually art. *Chronology* comes from the Latin word *chronologia*. I google that and discover it has something to do with time or arranging events in the order in which they occurred. It never fails. You look up one word and there is no end to where it takes you.

DeKlerk doesn't bother to ring the bell. He has the key to my grandfather's house, which he no doubt copied from the one he found under the back doormat last night. Hardly a historical object, but at least the chain of custody is clear. What is much less clear is the *provenance* of the three paintings no longer under Grandpa's bed.

It is not Rebecca who accompanies DeKlerk this time. But what is most astounding is the calmness with which he enters the house, as if he were an expected guest. Once inside the door, DeKlerk asks Zach to hold it open as he carefully pushes the wheelchair with its elderly occupant.

"My my, who are all of these charming young men?" the distinguished old woman asks. "Well, at least two of you seem quite charming. You, my dear young man, seem as if you had a serious encounter with someone's fist," she continues after looking more closely at Henry.

"I'm not sure I can account for all of them, Mrs. Bauer, but I have been introduced to this young man, Mr. Orphan's grandson, Robbie," DeKlerk answers, pointing to me. "I'm guessing that this older fellow, who slept so soundly during my visit last night, is Mr. Orphan's other grandson. This third gentleman is unknown to me."

"Are you kidding me? Did you break into this house last night?" Henry blurts out.

"Of course not! What an awful accusation, young man," DeKlerk answers. "I merely followed the instructions I was given by Mr. Orphan himself so that I might retrieve what rightfully belonged to Mrs. Bauer."

"What are you talking about? You know very well that my grandfather hasn't been able to talk to anyone since his stroke," I interrupt.

"Well, perhaps not since his stroke, but certainly prior to that," DeKlerk replies. "You know I met with your grandfather several days ago. He suffered that most untimely stroke after he returned home from that meeting. As I previously told you, Robbie, I was attempting to reunite your grandfather with a work of art that legally belongs to him. However, in turn, he offered to purchase three other small paintings from me, which belong to Mrs. Bauer. I secured the paintings for him in exchange for a promised fee. I never collected the payment and simply returned for Mrs. Bauer's property."

That's when I remember the partially made out check, the one for 150,000 dollars, not yet torn from Grandpa's checkbook. There was no name listed on the check, but the note on the memo line clearly said *Three Paintings.* Maybe this is all legitimate. But that is no excuse for DeKlerk to break into Grandpa's house.

"I don't know anything about any paintings, or who they belong to. I know you have no right to be in my grandfather's house," Henry declares with a seriousness that stuns me.

My brother, battered and bruised from who knows what, emerges from his typical unconscious state to take charge of the situation. He brushes past Zach, steps in front of me, and stands head to head with DeKlerk. Actually, now fully upright, Henry is at least a half a head taller than DeKlerk.

"What did you come back here for anyway? You have the paintings. What else do you want?" I ask.

"Apparently, we don't have the paintings," Mrs. Bauer asserts. "We have remarkably good copies of the paintings, but not the originals—at least not the ones Mr. DeKlerk gave your grandfather," the elderly woman continues.

Zach tries to get my attention with some hard to ignore eye-rolling and head movements. At first, I take the spasms to be nothing more than growing anxiety at the current circumstances. But when he doesn't relent, I realize he is signaling that I look at my phone. There is no way I can get to it without attracting notice from DeKlerk and the old woman. I need a distraction. And after almost 14 years, my big brother finally comes through for me. He vomits. He throws up all over DeKlerk's undoubtedly expensive, perfectly tailored three-piece suit.

With impressive precision and speed, Mrs. Bauer reverses her wheelchair just in time to avoid the flying slime. DeKlerk, not so lucky, takes a direct hit. I glance at the text. That's strange. It's coming from my grandfather's phone. It's our private signal, the one he uses when he wants me to come over as soon as possible, **WEES**. It was his idea, something about it being easy to remember and even easier to spell. I still don't know what it means, if it means anything.

Zach and I grab Henry and make our way to the back door. I retreat for just a moment to reach under the bed for the plastic bag containing the checkbook and letters. Perhaps once opened, they will reveal the *provenance* of the three paintings, and the true family ties that bind Grandpa to Bauer ancestry.

Chapter Seventeen
Remote Control

Grandpa always complains about new-fangled gadgets. I can hear him now. "How are you supposed to start a car without a key?" Precisely the question I ask as we climb into the unlocked van parked in Grandpa's driveway.

"Hang tight, little bro. I may be able to start this thing if the guy I just vomited on has the remote in his pocket," Henry says cautiously. He checks out the dashboard and locates the START button.

I glance anxiously at Zach in the back seat and twist around to see if anyone else is coming. Henry presses the button—nothing! DeKlerk emerges from the house; he is just close enough to trigger the remote—ignition! We are off as DeKlerk looks on in disbelief.

"Where to?" Henry asks a perfectly good question. He glances at the rearview mirror, backing out of the driveway at record speed. The problem is I have no good answer. Zach and I obviously are late for school. I have a text from Grandpa, or at least from his phone, signaling he needs to see me. And we have just stolen a van. There is clearly no good choice here.

Hearing no particularly helpful suggestion from me, Henry offers a possible plan, "I'm dropping you guys at school and ditching the van before someone reports it missing. I'll figure out a way to scope out Grandpa's house and get back in there. I don't think those two are going to hang around much longer."

Strangely, Henry is making sense for a change. With us gone and no sign of the original paintings at the house, there is no point in DeKlerk and Mrs. Bauer remaining at Grandpa's. I don't know what they will try next, but maybe Rebecca can help me get to the bottom of this. She was at Grandpa's with DeKlerk last night. She must know more about this. I have to get my hands on that letter, the one Rebecca insists was sent to Grandpa from his suspected brother.

"Are you in a trance or something, Robbie?" Zach calls out.

"I'm just trying to put the pieces together and figure out what to do next," I murmur.

"You guys better make up your minds because once I turn the engine off, I won't be able to restart the thing," Henry reminds us. "And I don't want to be driving around in this much longer."

"Drop us at school. We'll have to come up with some excuse for being late, but that's easier than trying to explain why we didn't show up at all," I declare.

Henry stops in front of West Hamilton Middle School. The street is eerily quiet, the steps leading up to the main entrance empty, all signaling that we are way beyond the first, second, and late bells. That means questions with few answers and some quick thinking. We need late passes to make it to what I am guessing is second-period social studies.

I hate to admit that I use Grandpa's stroke to my advantage, but in some strange way, that is the reason I am late. The excuse works rather well—not just for me, but for Zach too. The school secretary is so concerned about my grandfather that she barely pays attention to Zach.

Late passes in hand, we race to our lockers as the halls erupt with footsteps and voices. The third-period bell is barely noticeable above the clamor. Zach and I blend in as best we can, given the bizarre start to our day.

"I'll see you next period at lunch," Zach says. "Are you okay, Robbie?"

"I'm fine, I think. I'll see you next period," I answer.

There are two classes Zach and I don't have together, and third period is one of them. For the moment, I am relieved. I need to pull myself together and decide how to contact Rebecca again without DeKlerk and Mrs. Bauer finding out. I also have to make sense of Grandpa's text, if that even was from him. It was from his phone, and it was our private signal, *WEES*. There is so much flying around in my head that I hardly remember I am on my way to third-period English.

I get to the classroom only to find a note on the door.

Mr. Perlman's third-period class is meeting in the library.

I head to the stairwell and make my way up the two flights. A bit breathless, I notice the chairs have been moved from the individual tables and set up auditorium style. Mr.

Perlman steps to the front of the already seated students as I grab the last seat. Of course, my luck, it just happens to be in the first row so that all eyes are on me.

Mr. Perlman introduces the guest author, and I pretend to listen, something I have gotten pretty good at when my mind is on other things. With my eyes open just enough, and at precisely the right angle, I can pretty much convince any teacher I am paying attention.

Unfortunately, I forgot to leave my phone in the locker, a major violation at West Hamilton Middle School, and it starts vibrating nonstop. I get the look from Mr. Perlman and gently slip out of my seat, tiptoeing past the turning heads to the back of the library. Ms. Therasakapopulis, the shortest teacher in the school with the longest name steps from behind the school librarian's desk to block my exit.

"And just where are you going, Robbie?" she asks.

"Sorry about the phone, Ms. T. My grandfather is in the hospital. It's kind of an emergency," I reply.

"Okay, step outside and take the call, but be sure to see me before you go to your next class," she says.

Just what I need—detention, another explanation to Mom and Dad, and more delays in getting to Grandpa and Rebecca.

Not completely unexpected, the text is from Henry.

When are u done?
2:55 if I don't get detention, I answer.
Detention, that's my gig, not yours, Henry texts back.
Doing my best to keep up with my big bro, I reply.
Keep me posted!

I walk back into the library, take my seat, and resume my paying-attention stare. I glance at my watch—about 20 minutes to go—20 of the longest minutes of my entire life.

Finally, the bell rings, chairs get rearranged, kids make a mad dash for the front and rear exits, and Perlman and Therasakapopulis close in on me. A few stragglers look on sympathetically, or possibly gleefully, depending on just how many times they have been in the same predicament.

I brace myself for the attack. Perlman goes first. "We heard about your grandfather, Robbie. How's he doing?"

Ms. T. follows. "Robbie, is there anything we can do to help?"

This is not going so badly after all. I still feel a little guilty about using Grandpa's stroke to get me off the hook, but if it works, work it. That is what Henry always says. Great, now I am quoting my scheming brother.

I accept the reassuring words of my teachers, grateful I don't have to stay after school. Just as I get to the door, Ms. T. calls me back. I knew this was too good to be true.

"Robbie, there's something I forgot," Ms. T. says as she reaches into her desk to retrieve a book. "A student came all the way from Bellingham Prep to drop this off for you this morning. She said you had forgotten it at the Public Library and asked if I could give it to you. I believe she said her name was Rebecca," Ms. T. explains. "I had no idea you were interested in Sherlock Holmes, Robbie."

Chapter Eighteen
Special Delivery

Truth is I have no idea what Rebecca Bauer looks like. I could walk right past her in the hallway and never realize it. I have spoken to her. Zach has spoken to her. Henry was in the same room as her but managed to sleep through the whole thing. The fact is none of us have ever seen her.

I know DeKlerk is real. I know Mrs. Lillian Bauer exists. I know what both of them want me to believe. Rebecca has a different story to tell about my family. But without Grandpa, it is just another story.

I now hold a 752-page book in my hand, full of stories. If Rebecca is the real deal, then somewhere in this book is a letter from her grandfather, Nathan Bauer, to my grandfather, John Robert Orphan. I have a 40-minute lunch period to find out if anyone is telling the truth.

"You seem a bit startled, Robbie," Ms. T. observes.

"No, just surprised that someone went to the trouble."

"The young lady was quite determined to get this to you today," Ms. T. continues.

"Did she say anything else?"

"No, just wanted to make sure you got the book."

A thank you, several kind words about my grandfather's recovery, and I am on my way down to the cafeteria, Sherlock Holmes safely stowed in my backpack. Zach is at our usual table with Simon, Jake, Caleb, Rosa, and Sophie. He jumps up when he sees me. Subtlety is not his strong suit.

There is no way I can hang out here. I am in no mood to eat or talk. The only thing I can think about is the letter. And that is not something I want to share with anyone right now, not even Zach. The nurse's office might work. At least, it buys me some time and gives me an excuse to not go to my next class.

Zach's face says it all. He definitely is pissed. I don't blame him. He really has been there for me these past few days. I just need to check out this letter on my own.

It seems the whole school knows about my grandfather. The nurse offers to call my parents. That is the last thing I need right now.

"It's just a headache, Ms. Bennett," I explain. "Would it be okay if I just hang out here for a while? No need to bother my parents. They're pretty busy running back and forth to the hospital."

"Okay, Robbie. You can lie down in the next room. I'll check on you a little later."

Finally some privacy! I fumble with the zipper on the backpack, reach in, and pull out the book. My hands are actually shaking. I flip through the pages. A worn yellowed envelope, addressed to J.R. Bauer c/o John Robert Orphan, 120 Garfield Place, Brooklyn 15, New York, slips out. It is stamped *Addressee Unknown*. I read the postmark— *December 28, 1962*.

The envelope, back flap opened, begins to make sense of Rebecca's unseen voice. The letter is not the only thing in the envelope. There are three photos—one of two boys, one younger, one older; the second of a man and woman; and a third of all four surrounding a baby carriage. Something is handwritten on each of the photos—*Nathan und Jonathan, Mama und Papa, Bauer familie.* All are marked with the year—*1939.* The letter—written in English—begins with an apology.

My dear Broer,

Excuse my English. I send you these fotos, and hope you are well. I understand you wish not to answer my letters. I have written many. There are things we must settle while we remain living. You have a new life. So do I. We try not to remember. This too I understand. I feel much sorrow. You were so young and I did not protect you. I ask now for your forgiveness.

Nathan

I get why Rebecca is convinced we are related—second cousins, I guess, if our grandfathers were brothers. It may even explain why Grandpa refused to admit having a brother all these years. It is complicated, but if I have this family tree straight, why is Rebecca's grandmother denying that her husband and my grandfather were actually brothers? And where do DeKlerk and the stolen art fit into this?

There are about a dozen other sealed envelopes in the plastic bag in my backpack. Grandpa kept these but never opened them. I don't know what to do and there is only one person I trust to tell me.

"Robbie, how are you feeling?" Ms. Bennett says, peering through the door.

I quickly stuff everything into my backpack, "Much better."

"Great, because someone wants to check on you," she adds.

This is not rocket science. Ms. Bennett steps aside and Zach enters the room. He is not too forgiving. The look of exasperation from the cafeteria is now a fully formed angry stare.

"Are you really sick or what?" Zach demands.

"I read the letter, the one Rebecca tried to leave for me at the library," I explain.

"How did you get it?" Zach asks.

"Rebecca was here this morning before we got to school. She left it in the library with Therasakapopulis," I continue.

"What did it say?"

"Well, let's just say I understand why Rebecca thinks we're related."

"And?" Zach questions me further.

"And what?" I reply.

"And what does it have to do with the paintings, DeKlerk, and almost being held hostage this morning?" Zach exclaims, more loudly than I like with Nurse Bennett in the next room.

"Keep your voice down, Zach," I plead. "There is more we don't know than we know. I haven't heard from Henry since he dropped us off this morning. Rebecca managed to sneak in and out of here, and I still wouldn't know her if she were right in front of me."

I barely get my words out when my phone signals a text. Seems that Ms. Bennett thought it best to let Mom know I was not feeling well, after all. She is on her way to the hospital and is picking me up on the way there.

"Zach, this is going to piss you off even more, but my mom is picking me up in 15 minutes. I have to see my grandfather and figure out just how much to tell him if he'll even understand. It's the only way to put this puzzle together."

"Let me come with you, Robbie."

"You know that's not possible, Zach. There's no good reason for you to leave school early."

"Okay, but there is a good reason for me to walk you to the car."

"There is?"

"We wouldn't want someone in your weakened condition to walk down all those stairs by yourself," Zach says sarcastically.

I try to come up with a suitable response when the phone vibrates again, this time indicating a text from that all too familiar number.

"Who is it?" Zach asks.

"It's Rebecca," I whisper, somewhat stunned. "She's outside."

Chapter Nineteen
Cousins

There is a photo of Mom on the wall just outside of Grandpa's bedroom, probably taken when she was 11 or 12 years old. About a dozen other family photos surround it, but this is the one that usually catches my eye. Actually, I am not sure it is the photo or Grandpa's story about it that has always fascinated me. Let's just say that my mother's more rebellious side was revealed in the events that led up to the photo. Redheaded and freckle-faced, weighted down by a suitcase almost as big as herself, she stared intently at the photographer, my grandfather, not at all pleased that he had foiled her plan to run away.

Apparently, my mom's hair color set her apart from all other family members, proving she was, as she had always suspected, adopted. It took a bit of work unearthing her birth certificate and hospital records to convince her otherwise, but she eventually was persuaded. She was not adopted. Mom was born at University Hospital on July 4, 1970. And each year, when the red, white, and blue is patriotically on display, Grandpa pulls out her birth certificate and delights in the story about his runaway.

As I emerge from West Hamilton Middle School and finally set eyes on Rebecca Bauer, it is as if my mother's photo has come to life—red hair, freckles and all! I think we can dispense with a DNA test, not to mention DeKlerk's and Lillian Bauer's protests. Between the letter I just read and the remarkable physical resemblance to my mother, I have all the evidence I need. Rebecca and I are definitely related. So why would her grandmother deny it?

I race down the front steps of the building with Zach close behind. We almost collide as I come face to face with my newfound cousin Rebecca. The greeting is awkward at best, particularly when I remember that my mother is likely to drive up any minute.

"Rebecca?" I ask, despite knowing the answer.

She glances over my shoulder at Zach before responding. "Is there someplace we can talk?" she whispers.

"I don't think so. This is not a very good time. My mother is on her way here to pick me up."

"Correction," Zach interrupts, "Your mother has arrived."

There is no doubt about it. The distinct three-honk signal announces Mom's arrival even though the car is barely visible in the school's driveway.

"Well, it's your call. Do we include my mother in this or not?" I ask hesitantly.

"We can't. Not yet," Rebecca replies.

"I still don't get what all the secrecy is about, but unless you want to see exactly what you're going to look like in 30 years, you need to take off now!" I insist.

"What do you mean?" Rebecca asks.

"He means you could be Emily O'Neill's clone," Zach declares. "There's another way out of here across the athletic field. Follow me and we might just be able to avoid bumping into Robbie's mom."

That is something I wouldn't mind doing myself at the moment, but the next sound I hear after the horn honking is the text beeping. *Waiting in the driveway. Do u see me?* There is definitely no way out of this. Finally a face to face encounter with Rebecca, and I am no closer to finding out about Grandpa, stolen paintings, or my recently discovered extended family.

If there is any light at the end of this tunnel, it is what else I might learn from Grandpa himself. Mom and I are heading back to the hospital, and that is the best chance I have right now. As long as I don't get interrogated about the headache and my visit to the nurse, I can clear my brain and figure out what to do next. I just have to get Rebecca out of my head for now and hope Zach doesn't do anything dumb.

"I'm worried about you. First fainting in the elevator and now this headache. I know you're stressed about Grandpa, but what's going on, Robbie?" Mom asks.

I am staring at my mother while I think of something to say. Fainting was real. The headache was the excuse I needed to have a few minutes to read the letter. But I am not just staring because I don't have a clue about what to say to Mom. I still can't get over how much Rebecca and Mom look alike.

"How come nobody else in our family has red hair?" I blurt out.

"Are you trying to change the topic?" Mom answers, looking confused by my unexpected question.

That is not why I asked, but it does get us off of me for the moment. "No, I was just curious."

"I've had red hair my entire life, and certainly for the almost 14 years you know me, although it's getting grayer by the minute. Why are you asking now?"

"Never mind. Forget about it!" I snap.

Mom seems a bit startled by my sharp response and drops any discussion about my stress level and her hair. I usually don't do rude. That is Henry's turf. Mom is definitely caught off guard, and I immediately feel lousy. She has enough on her mind and no clue about what is on mine. The next several minutes pass in complete silence, as one traffic light after another turns green, permitting us to enter each intersection with hardly a pause. I owe Mom an apology, but don't want to invite any more questions I can't answer, or answer truthfully.

The parade of ambulances and police vehicles directly ahead signals our approach to the hospital. Mom drives past the emergency entrance to the visitors' parking lot. She pulls the ticket from the automatic dispenser. The machine's arm rises in salute as we take the ramp to the upper level.

Mom parks near the exit stairwell, turns off the ignition, and looks at me. "Are we okay?" she asks. "I realize we were both a little jumpy back there."

It is impossible to tell yourself to not think of something when it is the only thing you can think of. And while I hear Mom's voice, the only thing I can think about is Rebecca and how much she looks like the younger version of Mom. Thankfully, Mom is distracted by an incoming call, which from the sound of the ringtone, is from Dad.

"I just got here," Mom replies to Dad's obvious question. "Yes, Robbie is with me. Why? Is something wrong? When? How did it happen?"

All I hear is a string of questions with no clue about the answers on the other end. Mom hangs up. Her eyes well up with tears and I prepare myself for the worst.

"Grandpa is starting to say a few words. It's a little difficult to understand him, but he keeps making one point very clearly. He wants to see you, Robbie. The therapist is with him right now and is asking if you can join them."

"Sixth-floor West Neurology Unit, right?" I double check, grabbing my backpack and reaching for the door handle.

"Right, and please no fainting in the elevator. I'm going to grab a cup of coffee and meet you up there in a few minutes."

"Who contacted Dad, anyway?" I ask with one foot out the door.

"I guess the nurse or the therapist herself," Mom replies. "Actually, Dad said it was a he, not a she who called him. Grandpa's nurses are all women, so maybe there's a new male speech therapist working with him."

The chance to hear from Grandpa directly has me really pumped, so much so that I race into the stairwell that leads to the lobby and the main hospital elevator. I don't think about the white van at the opposite end of the upper parking level until I am halfway to the sixth floor.

Chapter Twenty
Knock on Wood

Sometimes a white van is just a white van. And sometimes a new male speech therapist is just a new male speech therapist. The image of the van registers in my brain but is quickly overpowered by the chance to talk to Grandpa. The elevator stops on the third and again on the fourth and fifth floors, letting visitors off and doctors on. Thankfully, it isn't too crowded, just slow. I step out on six and glance at the arrow directing me to the west wing of the neurology unit.

"Hey, Robbie. It is Robbie, right?" one of the nurses greets me.

I recognize Anna, the nurse my mother introduced me to the other day. "Yes. Can I see my grandfather now?"

"Sure. The speech therapist has been trying to contact someone from the family. Seems there's been a breakthrough, and your grandfather is anxious to see you," Anna explains.

"Is he alone?" I ask.

"His roommate went down for some tests a while ago. So it's just your grandfather and the therapist."

I follow Anna down the corridor. We pass several doors on the right and left when she extends her arm, inviting me to enter Grandpa's room. The privacy curtain is drawn, revealing only a pair of men's sneakers attached to whoever is sitting next to the bed.

"Excuse me. Robbie is here to see his grandfather," Anna announces as she steps back into the hallway.

With the curtain now partly open, I see Grandpa's familiar twisted smile. His gaze shifts from me to the young man now standing. Barely taller than me, and seemingly just past puberty, the only thing professional looking about Matt Russo is the name badge on his white coat.

"I know what you're thinking. I get this all the time. I only look like I'm 15. I am actually 28 and a fully licensed therapist. Your grandfather is in good hands," Matt assures me.

"It doesn't much matter to me how old you are, as long as you're not some middle-aged man with an accent," I declare.

"I don't get it," Matt responds.

"Never mind. Is my grandfather actually speaking?" I ask.

"Knock on wood. Knock on wood," Grandpa interrupts, more clearly than I might have expected, given our last attempt to communicate.

Matt turns toward Grandpa knowingly and gives him a thumbs up. "He has several familiar expressions, like the one you just heard. He uses them appropriately and that's a good start."

"I got a text from his phone earlier today. Is that something he would have been able to do by himself?" I inquire.

"No question there. He recognizes letters and words. He could easily tap out a text message with his good hand," Matt explains. "Are you okay telling me what he wrote to you?"

"It's just a signal between him and me. It's his way of letting me know he wants to see me. It doesn't mean anything to anyone else," I clarify.

"Is it **WEES**?"

"How do you know?"

"Because that was one of the other things he scribbled in his notebook that I couldn't make any sense of. Does your grandfather ever use another language?"

"Like what?" I ask.

"Like Dutch," Matt answers. "First I thought it might be an acronym, W.E.E.S., World Economic, etc., etc., etc., but it's not. **WEES** is Dutch for **ORPHAN**."

"I guess that's no big deal, given his last name," I reason.

"I was just curious about whether he spoke any other languages. It's not unusual for someone who has a stroke and aphasia to go back to his first language," Matt explains.

This is all very interesting for reasons I don't particularly want to go into with Matt, the speech therapist, right now. It is another puzzle piece that connects Grandpa to Amsterdam, stolen paintings, and a long lost brother.

Speaking of long lost brothers, I don't have a clue where mine is or has been for the past several hours. I don't know where Zach and Rebecca went after they managed to avoid Mom. And last but not least, I don't know what DeKlerk's and Mrs. Bauer's next moves are likely to be.

"I have a few more patients to see this afternoon," Matt announces. "Hang out with your grandfather for a while. I'll stop by before I leave for the day."

Mom walks into the room just as Matt turns to leave. She is no less surprised by the boyish appearance of the speech therapist than I was. After introductions and Matt's explanation for leaving, she looks to Grandpa and me for some sign of progress.

"How's it going, Dad?"

"Hold your horses. Hold your horses," Grandpa repeats.

"That's one of those familiar phrases your father is able to use now," Matt clarifies for Mom.

"Wow, that was pretty good. I guess things are better," Mom declares. "Are you asking us to be patient, Dad?"

Grandpa nods affirmatively and closes his eyes. Anna steps into the room and suggests we let Grandpa get some rest. She directs us to a lounge, which at the moment is fully occupied by patients and their visitors.

Mom and I agree on the cafeteria as an alternative. We are almost at the elevator when I realize I left my backpack in the room.

"I don't think you need to worry about it, Robbie. I'm sure the backpack is safe in Grandpa's room. You can get it when we come back up later," Mom assures me.

There is no way I am letting it out of my sight, not with its current contents. "Go ahead, Mom. I'll meet you at the elevator in a second."

I dash back to find Grandpa dozing off and step into the room as quietly as possible. A bit startled by my return, he opens his eyes and simply repeats, "Knock on wood. Knock on wood."

"I didn't mean to wake you, Grandpa. I just came to get my backpack. Get some rest. Mom and I will be back later," I promise.

"No, no," Grandpa says, carefully forming each syllable. "Just you!"

"That's not going to be easy. You know Mom," I remind him.

There are so many questions I have and answers my grandfather might be able to give me now. But with Mom just down the hall and likely to come looking for me any minute, I assure Grandpa I will try.

The words are more strained this time and spoken with new emphasis, "Knock on wood. Knock on wood!"

Sometimes a white van is just a white van. And sometimes a new male speech therapist is just a new male speech therapist. But sometimes an expression is not just an expression. Grandpa is trying to tell me something, but what?

Chapter Twenty-One
Charlie

Grandpa's words echo in my head but offer little else for me to go on. I grab my backpack and make my way to the elevator and Mom. The earlier tension between us gone, we share some small talk about school on our way down to the cafeteria. Fortunately, I am able to dodge any risky questions and haven't said anything to arouse her suspicion.

Then, predictably, Mom brings up Henry. I have a well-rehearsed answer about my brother's whereabouts, anticipating she would get to this topic sooner or later. But rather than ask, she informs me.

"Henry texted a few minutes ago," Mom explains.

"Really? I mean really," I reply, quickly shifting the tone of my voice.

"You know that I know that he never went back to school," Mom says very matter-of-fact like. "It's about time that your father and you stop trying to protect me from the trouble your brother has a habit of getting himself into."

I am about to offer my version of Henry's planned return to school when Mom reveals the rest of what she knows. Surprisingly, she is aware of his not so well-concealed bruises and his brief stay at Grandpa's house. What she is clueless about is the part I played.

"Where is Henry now?" I ask innocently.

"I was hoping you could tell me," Mom replies.

"How would I know?" I answer with a question.

"I'm not sure, Robbie, but I have a feeling you know more about what's going on with Henry than you're admitting," Mom concludes.

This may actually work. Mom is focused on Henry. What else is new? But that could be just the distraction I need so I can figure out my next move.

"What did Henry's text say?" I ask.

"Just that he is okay and not to worry. What he really wanted to know is where you are."

That doesn't make any sense. Why isn't Henry contacting me directly? It has never been easy to figure out why Henry does most things. But this seems strange.

"Did you tell him I am with you at the hospital?" I ask.

"I did. Is that a problem?" Mom answers.

"Of course not," I say. Still curious about why he is asking Mom and not me, I am relieved at the same time. He must have dumped the white van by now and at least DeKlerk is not holding him captive. But for some reason, he is avoiding my phone.

Why would Henry avoid my phone? He wouldn't! But someone other than Henry, trying to track me down, might. That leaves two possibilities.

"Mom, can I see your phone?"

"Why?" she asks, looking somewhat puzzled.

"I just want to see what time Henry texted you," I explain. But what I really want to see is if the text actually came from Henry's phone. It did, which rules out the first possibility. But it didn't come from Henry, which rules in the second possibility.

Whoever sent the text signed it, *Henry*, and that is something my big brother never does. He never signs his texts! That may be too subtle for Mom's detection, but not mine.

My best hope is Henry not only dumped the van, he left his phone in it on purpose. My best guess is DeKlerk has the van back, with my brother's phone as a bonus. That means he can keep track of me, but it also means I can keep track of him.

With the dinner hour approaching, the hospital cafeteria begins to fill up. Mom and I settle at one of the few remaining tables close to the entrance. She asks me to keep an eye on her bag while she gets us something to eat. More importantly, she leaves her phone on the table as she heads to the growing line of hospital personnel and visitors waiting to be served.

I recheck the text from Henry's phone and examine the tracking app. The text was sent at 4:36 pm, just about an hour ago. As for the phone's location, Belmont Avenue, between Northridge and Highland Boulevards, most definitely the high rent district, and certainly nowhere Henry would be hanging out.

The chatter and shuffling of chairs and trays make it difficult to concentrate, particularly with Mom likely to return any minute. The rising noise level almost blocks out the whispered calling of my name. The third time I hear something that sounds like "Robbie," I look up to see Henry at the entrance several feet away.

I decide to dispense with the *Do you know that I know that Mom knows* line of questioning and cut right to the chase. "Where have you been since this morning and how did you get here?"

"I dropped the van off in the parking lot behind the post office on Sutter Avenue. I figured DeKlerk, or whatever his name is, would locate it easily. He must have one of those parking apps on his phone. It served our purpose, getting us out of there this morning, and holding him and the old lady off for a while," Henry explains.

"Did you leave your…" I start but am interrupted mid-question by Mom's return.

"Well, well, the prodigal son returns," Mom says, unusually sarcastic. "Did you think you could skip town without me finding out what you were really up to?"

Seems Emily O'Neill is getting a little more real about her eldest son. There may be hope for her yet. Although, truth be told, Henry has come through for me today in ways I never would have imagined possible.

"Could I just get something to eat now and talk later?" Henry asks.

"You guys share the sandwiches. I'll get something else for myself. Just don't go anywhere until you tell me where you've been and what happened to your face, Henry," Mom says.

It may be just a few minutes, but Mom's return to the even longer cafeteria line gives Henry and me the time to fill each other in.

Realizing where I was going with my earlier question, Henry continues. Yes, he left his phone in the van deliberately. No, he had no idea where Zach was. Where was he since he dropped us off at school this morning? Grandpa's house!

"You went back there? Are you crazy? What if DeKlerk and the old lady were still there? Were they?" I ask in rapid-fire succession.

"I scoped out the place pretty carefully before going back into the house," Henry assures me.

"And…?"

"And that's when I bumped into Charlie."

"Charlie Wood? Grandpa's neighbor?"

"He stopped me on the way in to see how Grandpa was doing. He was visiting his kids in Ohio for a few days and just got back. He heard about Grandpa's stroke and asked if he could visit him in the hospital. He wanted to know how I got the black eye."

"Henry, just get to the point before Mom gets back," I plead.

"He told me Grandpa gave him a package the day he left to see his kids, something he asked Charlie to hold onto until he organized some things in the basement. That must have been the day before Grandpa's stroke."

That's when it hits me. *Knock on wood*! *Charlie Wood*!

"The real paintings?" I ask hopefully.

Mom is back. And I never get my answer.

Chapter Twenty-Two
Belmont Avenue

Mom has Henry and me just where she wants us, together and in plain sight. One thing is certain; the questions are about to start. What is less certain is how we keep from answering them. For this, I rely on Henry's unmatched skill at diversion.

"I know you know I've been hanging out at Grandpa's," Henry says before Mom has a chance to ask.

"Well, I know you're in some kind of trouble and didn't go back to school," Mom declares.

"You remember Grandpa's neighbor, Charlie?" Henry asks, cleverly changing the subject.

"What does he have to do with not going back to school? And before you make up some story we both know is not true, why don't you tell me what happened to your face?" Mom insists.

It looks like Mom is winning this round and not letting Henry off the hook for a change. Henry's purplish bruises begin to turn an interesting shade of red. To my amazement, he is actually stuck.

Just when this gets good, Mom's phone sounds off with Dad's identifiable ring, and Henry catches a momentary break. After telling Dad she is in the cafeteria with the boys, Mom nods her head. She repeats "Okay" three times, and Henry and I are left, trying to figure out what she is agreeing to.

"Why did you want to know about Grandpa's neighbor, Charlie?" Mom asks Henry.

"Because I bumped into him. He just got back from visiting his kids and asked about Grandpa," Henry replies.

"Is that all?" Mom continues.

"Why? What did Dad say?" I interrupt.

"Charlie called the house to see where Grandpa was. He seemed pretty upset when he heard about the stroke and insisted on coming to the hospital to see him," Mom explains. "Dad asked if I thought Grandpa could have a visitor."

"And you agreed?"

"I don't see why not. Grandpa is stable and it might do him some good to see an old friend."

Actually, it might do me some good for Grandpa to see an old friend who may be in possession of the very paintings that DeKlerk is so anxious to get his hands on. And it will certainly do Henry some good to get out of answering any more of Mom's questions.

Henry and I stand up, push our chairs back, and collect the cafeteria trays. I hoist my backpack onto my shoulder. I am not sure what he is thinking. I know I have to get back up to Grandpa's room. With no word from Zach and Rebecca and no clue about DeKlerk's next likely move, Charlie's visit may be my best hope.

"And just where do you think you guys are going?" Mom calls out.

"I don't know about Henry, but I'm going back up to Grandpa," I answer.

"I don't think so. You're both going home. Henry still has quite a bit of explaining to do, and you no doubt have homework. You'll see Grandpa tomorrow after school," Mom announces. "Dad will take you home after he drops Charlie off to see Grandpa."

"That's cool, but Dad doesn't need to go back and forth. I'll get Robbie home safe and sound. You have my word," Henry promises.

What do the look on Mom's face and my thoughts have in common with Henry's promise? One small shred of hope that he comes through for all of us!

The elevator stops on the main floor where Mom has arranged to meet Dad and Charlie. Polite greetings and Henry goes into a quick-talking mode. He convinces Dad to hang out and drive home with Mom later. Dad's car keys in hand, Henry escorts me to the parking lot. I am still unsure what he has up his sleeve, but I am feeling something I have never felt before—confidence in my big brother.

"I know we're not going home, but exactly what do you have in mind?" I ask.

"Check your tracking app," Henry directs. "Are you still getting a signal from my phone?"

I reach into my backpack, grab my phone, and check. "No change in the past hour, Belmont Avenue between Northridge and Highland Boulevards," I report.

"The problem is that if we know where DeKlerk is, he knows where we are and that we've left the hospital," Henry reasons. "Turn off the app!"

Fumbling with the setting, I remember I can use the app to check Zach's location. I don't know why I didn't think of that earlier.

"What are you doing?" Henry asks.

"Trying to locate Zach," I answer.

"Not now, Robbie. I'm sure he's fine. No news is good news, and if you haven't heard from him since you left school, let it go," Henry cautions.

"I can't let it go. Zach is my best link to Rebecca, and Rebecca is my best lead to whatever is going on with Grandpa," I explain.

"There are still things I clearly don't know or understand about Rebecca's connection to Grandpa, but if it takes Zach to figure it out, which is hard for me to believe, go for it," Henry concedes. "Where is he?"

A sudden clap of thunder and the skies open up. The deafening sound of the pouring rain makes it almost impossible to hear Henry. I'm not even sure he can see where he is going as the sheets of water wash over the windshield. We pull over to the nearest curb as the phone signal goes in and out. I watch the circling icon, waiting for the phone to show me Zach's location.

"Well, where is he?" Henry repeats, raising his voice.

Finally, the little dot on the screen settles on a street. "Belmont Avenue, between Northridge and Highland Boulevards," I answer.

"What's there?" Henry asks.

"Not what, who. That's the last location I have for your phone, the one you left in the white van," I explain. "Seems like Zach and Rebecca managed to work their way back to DeKlerk and the old lady. The question is why?"

"We're not going to get any answers sitting here," Henry offers. "Let's just hope your dorky buddy knows what he's doing."

"Let's hope so," I echo.

Zach is not the most logical person I know, but he is definitely the most cautious. If Rebecca persuaded him to follow her back to DeKlerk and her grandmother, there must be a good reason.

The rain slows down, Henry starts the ignition, and we take off. "You turned off the tracking app?" Henry confirms. "If we're heading to Belmont Avenue, there is no point in announcing our arrival!"

Chapter Twenty-Three
One Picture Is Worth
A Thousand Words

It turns out Belmont is not a where. It is a what. Belmont Avenue is a forever-winding street that runs right through the city. It starts in the old industrial part of town, where the factories have been converted to loft apartments and fancy boutique shops. It goes through the downtown business district and ends just outside the city limits in the east end lake area. These are not just homes; they are mini-mansions surrounded by sprawling acres of green and gated driveways that never seem to end.

The rain stops, the sky brightens, and even though it is close to dusk, there is enough light to make out the engraving on the stone wall as we cross the intersection of Belmont and Northridge, *Belmont Estates Senior Community*.

"What is this?" I ask.

"Looks like a very pricey old age home to me," Henry replies.

"Are you sure we're at the right place?"

"This is the only Belmont Avenue I know, and it's the only block between Northridge and Highland Boulevards.

What's more, there's a white van parked at the end of the driveway," Henry observes.

"DeKlerk's van?"

"At least according to the tracking app. And if the old lady lives here, that's a pretty safe bet," Henry reasons.

It doesn't take long for us to figure out we can't just walk through a locked security gate, knock on the front door, introduce ourselves, and ask for Mrs. Lillian Bauer. In fact, if we park here much longer, we're bound to attract unwanted attention.

"What now?" I ask.

"I don't know if Zach is in there, and whether or not Rebecca is with him. I do know we're not hanging around much longer to find out," Henry declares.

"So what are we doing?"

"We're going home before Mom and Dad send out a search party. We're getting on the computer and finding out exactly what this place is. And that's not all, Robbie."

"It's not?"

"No, it's not. You're going to come clean and tell me what you know about where Grandpa was the night of the stroke and what you found at his house."

Henry is making sense, which still is surprising. But what doesn't make sense is how Zach ended up here and what he and Rebecca are up to. I can text him, but that could tip off DeKlerk.

"Zach has gone out on a limb for me these past few days. I can't just abandon him, Henry."

It isn't an argument. It's more like a debate as we consider the pros and cons of leaving. And with time running out, two simultaneous texts pretty much decide for us.

Dad to Henry, *Where r u? no answer at home.* Zach to me, *Where r u? new intel about DeKlerk.*

Zach, the spy, now obviously thinks he is working for the CIA. I admire his persistence and certainly his loyalty, but Henry is literally in the driver's seat. He has the car, but I have my feet.

"Go home, Henry. I'm not leaving until I find out what's going on in there."

"You're nuts, little brother. I'm not leaving you here alone."

"And I'm not leaving Zach here. I don't know what he thinks he found out, but if it has anything to do with Grandpa, I'm not going anywhere."

"You're risking getting Mom and Dad more involved in this," Henry warns.

"That's where you get to put your talents to good use. You'll think of something," I reply.

"Okay, but for right now, we have to move this car before someone gets suspicious."

Henry and I devise a plan, which is immediately thwarted by the wailing of the sirens approaching from both sides of Belmont Avenue. Ours is no longer the only car on the street. The gate to *Belmont Estates Senior Community* swings open as an ambulance and two police emergency vehicles enter the grounds.

In the chaos of the next several minutes, a number of the estate's occupants emerge, some on foot supported by canes and walkers, others in wheelchairs accompanied by staff.

Among them are Zach and the now recognizable Rebecca, bent almost in half and gasping for breath.

I jump out of the car, wave my arms frantically to get their attention and rush them into the back seat. Henry takes full advantage of the confusion and steps on the gas just as police begin to block the street with yellow caution tape.

"Are you okay? What happened?" Henry and I ask in unison.

"We're okay," Zach says between choking coughs. "I don't know what happened, some sort of gas leak, I think."

"Accident or deliberate?" Henry wonders aloud.

"I doubt it was an accident," Rebecca concludes. "But it sure was a good way to empty out the place in a hurry."

"What is this place and what were you doing here?" I ask.

"It's a long story, most of which I'll get to later," Zach replies. "Actually, Rebecca can explain it better than me. Let's just say it's been an interesting few hours since we left school."

"I showed up at your school to leave the letter for you, but when the situation became more urgent, I knew we had to meet in person," Rebecca adds.

"What situation?" I ask, more baffled by the minute.

The only person more confused than me at the moment is Henry. He is looking at us as if we're speaking in code. Deliberation complete, the decision is made to drive to Grandpa's for the debriefing. Henry is tasked with the challenge of dealing with Mom and Dad, as well as Zach's parents. Rebecca is convinced that no one will be looking for her any time soon—explanation to follow. Oh, and one more thing, Zach managed to conduct some surveillance back at *Belmont Estates Senior Community*.

Stopped at an intersection and barely able to see the blurred images on Zach's phone in the darkness, he describes the collection of paintings on the video he recorded in the estate's basement.

"What am I looking at?" I ask.

"You're looking at a cache of artwork systematically stolen over decades—artwork never returned to their rightful owners—artwork believed to have been destroyed during World War II," Rebecca explains.

"What is it doing in an old age home?" Henry asks.

"Let's just say there are elderly people who live at Belmont, but it is anything but an old age home," Rebecca offers.

Chapter Twenty-Four
Art History

Zach's go-to expression any time anyone wants to know about anything—*search it up*! Equipped with smartphones and our combined digital expertise, the four of us, well three of us with Henry driving and his phone still in the white van, get to work. Battery power at a premium and no obvious place to recharge, we divide the search, *Nazi stolen art, World War II art return, Belmont Estates Senior Community*.

Tons of stuff comes up about the Nazis, stolen art, and efforts to compensate legitimate owners. Nothing comes up about Belmont, at least not the old age home. But what does come up is *The Belmont Project*, and its director, *Josef DeKlerk*.

Zach shouts out something from a newspaper article about an agreement signed in 1998 to return confiscated art to victims of Nazi persecution. There is a whole list of galleries and private collectors who were unaware that they were in possession of art stolen during World War II.

But it is Rebecca's search into *The Belmont Project* that is most revealing, not for what it mentions, rather for what it does not mention. It says nothing about art. Authorized by various governments in Europe, Israel, and the United States, its purpose is to identify and reunite family members who were separated during World War II.

Rebecca reads aloud from the website—*Due to the significant reduction of remaining Holocaust survivors, The Belmont Project has been discontinued. Information regarding reunification of families separated during the war should be addressed to the United States Holocaust Memorial Museum, Washington D.C.*

"The Belmont Project was a hoax," Rebecca declares. "If it reunited anyone, it was for one purpose and one purpose only, to line DeKlerk's pockets. And my grandmother and your grandfather were to be the next victims."

"Do you think the old man, sorry, I mean Grandpa, knew what DeKlerk was up to?" Henry asks.

"He suspected something. I'm convinced of that. It's just that he can't tell us much more right now," I respond.

"No, but my grandmother has information which could clear things up," Rebecca interrupts.

"Your grandmother? I don't think so. Isn't she the one who insists that you and I are not related, that our grandfathers weren't actually brothers? She seemed pretty cozy with DeKlerk last I saw," I add.

"Okay, now you've really lost me. Who is related to whose grandfather?" Henry asks. "And don't anyone say it's a long story. Just tell me who is who, and why I should care."

"You or me?" Rebecca asks.

"Why don't you give it a shot? I still don't know if I really get it all," I confess.

Rebecca uses the remaining time it takes to get to Grandpa's house to introduce herself to her other cousin. She shares the deceased Nathan Bauer's story, recently unearthed among his papers after his death. She explains that Nathan Bauer and John Robert Bauer were brothers, separated during the war.

What is left unknown is why John Robert Bauer changed his name to Orphan and concealed his true identity from his family. The other piece, of course, now open only to speculation, is why Lillian Bauer—Nathan's widow, Rebecca's grandmother—denies the two men were brothers.

"It doesn't take a genius to figure that out," Zach finally chimes in. "That has to be on DeKlerk. When did he enter the picture?"

"After my grandfather died. Well, actually before he died," Rebecca mumbles. "My grandfather never really got used to the computer. I handled most of his emails. DeKlerk reached out to him about three months before he died."

"Anything make you suspicious?" Zach continues.

"Not really. DeKlerk was interested in my grandfather's experiences as a survivor. When he was younger, my grandfather never went near the topic. But as he got older and frail, that's all he wanted to talk about," Rebecca answers. "It all seemed pretty innocent until after his death."

"What changed?" Henry asks as he pulls into Grandpa's driveway.

"My father was transferred from New York to his company's San Francisco office. My parents went to California for several weeks to find a house and get things set up for our move. I stayed back to finish the school year, keep my grandmother company, and help her sort through and pack her things."

"If she was going with you guys, how did she wind up at Belmont?" I ask.

"That was DeKlerk," Rebecca answers.

"You mean he just showed up one day?" Henry inquires.

"I answered one of his emails and told him my grandfather died. He asked if he could pay his respects and visit. That's the first we heard about stolen art that belonged to my grandfather's family."

"And your parents agreed to his coming?" Zach asks.

"My mother was skeptical, but my father convinced her that it was my grandmother's decision. DeKlerk showed up about a week after my parents left—sophisticated, well dressed, polite, and very official. And that's when things changed."

The rest of Rebecca's tale is predictable. Going through her grandfather's papers, she became aware of his previously unknown brother. DeKlerk discredited any possible relationship, convincing Mrs. Bauer of the existence of stolen art, which was legally hers, and hers alone.

More importantly, in a matter of two weeks and several visits, DeKlerk persuaded the elderly woman to consider remaining among friends and moving to *Belmont Estates Senior Community* rather than San Francisco. Certainly, she didn't want to become a burden to her son and daughter-in-law when she could live independently in familiar surroundings. While she has not yet agreed to his proposal, she now spends afternoons there getting acquainted with its residents.

There is not much any of us can say after a story like that. The question is what to do next. Stunned by what we are hearing, we get out of the car and go into Grandpa's, this time unlocking and walking through the front door. We haven't quite resolved how to handle Mom and Dad, Zach's mother, and now Rebecca's parents, but we're working on it.

"Was your grandmother at Belmont this afternoon?" I ask.

"She was supposed to be, but then remembered an appointment with her lawyer to discuss the possible move to Belmont. She pleaded with me to not tell my parents until after she met with the attorney. That's when I realized things were moving way too fast, and I had to speak to you," Rebecca explains.

No sooner are we inside Grandpa's house, than another car pulls into the driveway next door. Mom and Dad arrive with Charlie. My heart stops. Zach grabs Rebecca for their second escape of the day and heads toward the basement.

"Wait, my parents are going to see the car and realize we're here. Maybe it's time to read them in on all of this," I suggest reluctantly.

"That won't be necessary," the accented voice calls from Grandpa's bedroom. "I didn't bring the van this time; the taxi was more convenient and much more difficult to track. I'm happy to escort your friends to the basement while you figure out what to do with your parents," DeKlerk announces.

"What makes you think we will let you escort us anywhere, Mr. DeKlerk?" Rebecca asks.

"Oh, I've acquired a fair amount of insurance where that's concerned, young lady," DeKlerk warns, pressing a gun to Zach's temple.

"Are you crazy? What are you doing?" Rebecca cries out.

"I'm in no mood to be tested by you and your new-found acquaintances. Forewarned is forearmed. The two of you get down these stairs. And you, young Robbie, lest you doubt my intentions, consider carefully what you and your brother tell your parents."

Chapter Twenty-Five
Multiples of Three

Maybe it's just superstition, but I have this thing about the number three. I wouldn't say it's my lucky number, but it is a number that turns up a lot in my life. Sometimes it is actually the number three; other times it is a multiple of three. My birthday is the third day of the third month of the year. There are six letters in my first name and six letters in my last name. When important things happen that don't involve threes, I figure out a way to connect them to the number three anyway. There are four of us in my family. But if you count our dog, Luke, and cat, Luna, there are actually six.

I can get pretty hung up about connecting important events in my life to the number three, maybe even a little obsessive at times. But right now, there are three people in the basement of my grandfather's house at 699 Dorchester, and three unaccounted for paintings that may be hidden in Charlie Wood's house next door. Mom, Dad, and Charlie, a total of three people, are about to enter Charlie's house, but certainly not before noticing Dad's BMW X3 parked in Grandpa's driveway.

DeKlerk follows Rebecca and Zach down the basement stairs and closes the door, his threats echoing in my head. Having never been that close to an actual gun before, I can't get the image out of my mind. Henry and I jostle for position, the doorbell rings, not once or twice, but three times. I draw the short straw and let my parents in without a clue about what to do next.

"What are you guys doing here?" Mom asks, and Dad repeats a second later.

"I came to pick up some things I left here last night," Henry replies nervously. Not the best explanation, but better than anything I might come up with under the circumstances and hopefully enough to satisfy Mom and Dad for now.

"Well, since you're here, you can help us get some of Grandpa's things together. He's not going to be able to stay by himself anytime soon," Mom explains. "He's either going to a rehab facility or moving in with us for a while after he gets out of the hospital."

"Sure, Mom. What do you need us to do?" I ask.

"One of you needs to go next door. Charlie said Grandpa left a package there and someone needs to pick it up," Dad interjects. "I guess you can take care of that, Robbie. Henry, you come down to the basement with me. Grandpa's got a couple of suitcases down there. We'll need those to pack up his things."

There is no doubt anyone within three feet of me—which is just about where my parents are standing—can hear the pounding in my skull. The sound is so loud, I know my heart has permanently relocated from my chest to my head.

"I've got it, Dad. Let me take care of the suitcases," Henry declares.

"I appreciate your help, but you're not going to know where to look. It's an absolute mess down there. Grandpa's a bit of a collector. There are decades of files and all sorts of tchotchkes all over the place," Dad explains.

And then, barely noticeable with the pounding in my head, three clicks. The basement door is locked from the inside with DeKlerk, Rebecca, and Zach all below. Three clicks for the three locks Grandpa installed because of our shared superstition. But the good thing is that once locked, it takes a key to open the door from inside or out.

"Come on, Henry. Give me a hand," Dad insists.

Now it is Henry's turn to panic as Dad passes between us to get to the basement door. He grabs hold of the doorknob, jiggles it, and realizes the door is locked.

"Do you have the keys?" Dad asks Mom.

"Grandpa doesn't usually lock it," Mom answers. "Are you sure you can't open it?"

"No, he must have locked it that night when he went out," Dad says after another attempt at the doorknob.

"Robbie, check the kitchen drawer where Grandpa usually keeps his keys," Mom requests.

I seize upon the word *usually* for my out. Whether it was DeKlerk or not, someone locked the basement door from the inside with the keys that hang from a hook on the wall at the top of the stairs. That leaves two more sets, three sets of three keys in all. With me in possession of a second set, not here, but in my desk at home, there is a strong possibility that the third set is indeed in Grandpa's kitchen drawer.

I now face the likelihood that I have to tell another lie, something I gave up a few days ago. I make my way to the kitchen when the image of the plastic bag retrieved from the hospital containing Grandpa's stuff comes into focus. There were keys in that bag. Is it too much to hope for?

I open the drawer slowly in silent prayer and hold my breath. I really don't want to tell another lie. The pounding in my head subsides a bit, and I resume breathing. The third set of keys is not there!

Somewhat disappointed, but also certain that there will be another opportunity to retrieve Grandpa's suitcases, Dad moves on to the next item on his agenda. He reminds me about the package in Charlie's house and suggests that he and Mom head home for some well-deserved rest.

"No more stops, guys. Pack up whatever you left here last night, Henry. Get the package from Charlie and home. I want us all under the same roof. We have some talking to do and some planning about how to handle the next steps for Grandpa."

Mom seems to have something else on her mind. She is about to pick up on her investigation into Henry's bruises and last night's disappearing act.

"Not now," Dad pleads. "You're exhausted. I'm exhausted. We'll deal with this later at home."

"Okay, but I do eventually want some answers, Henry," Mom agrees reluctantly.

Dad holds the front door open and motions for me to go first. He escorts Mom down the steps to her car parked in Charlie's driveway. I listen for the engine just to be sure neither of them decides to double back for another check of the basement keys. No need to knock. Charlie opens his door in anticipation of my arrival.

There is nothing Charlie would like more than to strike up a conversation about his recent visit with his kids in Ohio. I try not to be rude, but there is simply too much going on next door for me to hang out and be polite.

"Let me get your grandfather's package," Charlie says, realizing he doesn't have my full attention.

"I'd love to hear about your visit, Mr. Wood, but Henry and I really need to get home," I say apologetically.

"Sure, sure, Robbie. Give me a minute."

Charlie takes a key from his wallet. He shuffles more than he walks toward a closet in the hall between the living room and back bedroom. He opens it, reaches up to the top shelf, and removes three brown paper wrapped squares, virtually identical to the ones I found the other night under Grandpa's bed.

"Do you know what these are?" Charlie asks.

"I'm not sure," I reply hesitantly. "Do you?"

"Some things your grandfather tells me. Some things he keeps to himself. He asks me to do him a favor. I do it, no questions asked," Charlie discloses. "The man has a lot of secrets, things from his past he won't talk about."

Charlie Wood probably knows more about Grandpa than he realizes. It's just not a conversation I can have right now. I'm also not about to march back into Grandpa's house with the very thing that DeKlerk is after. I don't know what he might have overheard from his vantage point in the basement. I only pray Zach and Rebecca are unharmed.

Dad's car is unlocked. I open the trunk and carefully place the three wrapped squares inside. I enter Grandpa's house to find the basement door open, Henry having joined the others below. The voices are muffled at first, but an argument is apparent.

"Just what do you think you're doing?" Henry shouts.

"Looking for Lillian Bauer's property," DeKlerk fires back.

"There is nothing down here that belongs to my grandmother," Rebecca insists. "And even if there is, you would see to it that she never gets it, Mr. DeKlerk."

"A contemptible, but somewhat accurate accusation," DeKlerk proclaims. "I attempted to assist the old woman, and had Mr. Orphan not suffered a stroke, this business would have all been concluded by now."

"Seems the only one you assisted is yourself," I announce from the top of the basement stairs. "But if it's the three paintings you're after, I know where they are now."

"Why the change of heart, young man?" DeKlerk asks cautiously.

Henry looks at me in disbelief. It takes a moment for him to catch my drift. It's been years since we hung out in the basement at 699 Dorchester, not with Grandpa, but with Grandma. It's been six years since she died and at least that long since her basement workshop was left untouched and locked in her memory.

"Follow me, Mr. DeKlerk," I say, descending the basement stairs. "I think I may know where the authentic paintings are hidden."

"What are you doing?" Rebecca and Zach shout simultaneously.

"Putting an end to this," I whisper as I try to recall the combinations and unlock the workshop door.

"Do you remember the combinations?" Henry asks.

"Two locks this time, each with its own combination. First lock—12 to the right, 9 to the left, 18 to the right; second lock—reverse the order of the numbers. All multiples of three!"

Chapter Twenty-Six
A Formidable Adversary

Grandpa's favorite meal is bagels and *lox*, nothing he will be eating anytime soon. It just pops into my head. I remember the first time I heard him say it when he invited us for breakfast one Sunday morning. My reply, *locks are for doors, not for eating.* Another one of those challenges of the English language, words that sound the same, but have two meanings.

Funny, the things you think of at the weirdest times. I coax DeKlerk into Grandma's long-sealed workshop with the promise of the three paintings he covets, and I'm thinking about *lox*. Actually, I'm thinking about how to slip past him once he's inside so I can set the combinations on the *locks* and detain him long enough to find Rebecca's grandmother.

DeKlerk enters the room slowly, his gun protruding ominously from its holster. He is anxious to get his hands on the paintings, yet doubtful about my surrender to his threats. For the moment and somewhat surprisingly, he leaves Rebecca, Zach, and Henry unattended in the larger basement area.

The ten-foot square room is exactly as I remember it, other than the dust-covered surfaces and cobwebbed corners. Family photos hang on the papered walls, accompanied by faded outlines where others were removed. There is a writing table still strewn with Grandma's papers. On top of a pile of yellow lined pads is an old Smith-Corona electric typewriter, the one Grandma refused to exchange for a computer. A ceiling fan is suspended above the table, one of its four blades missing. I can almost picture her at work, welcoming any interruption by Henry or me.

"The paintings better be here," DeKlerk threatens, as he scans the space.

"It's the only logical place my grandfather would have hidden them," I answer.

"But you're not certain?"

"No, but if the paintings are in the house, trust me, this is where they are."

"I doubt either of us trusts the other, young man. You may think you are a formidable adversary, but by now you must realize you are outmatched," DeKlerk warns.

"Help me move this cabinet. My guess is the paintings are in the wall safe behind it," I reply.

"I think not. Get your big brother to assist," DeKlerk commands. "I'm not foolish enough to turn my back on you."

"Henry is pretty banged up," I argue.

"Then get your friend to help," DeKlerk orders.

"Zach, I need your help with this," I call out.

Zach approaches us cautiously and follows my lead without protest. We push the cabinet away from the wall, revealing what DeKlerk believes to be a safe. As I rotate the dials, first in one direction, and then the other, a click signals the locks' release. With the door open just enough for us to fit, I grab Zach by the arm and push him through the opening. We pull the cabinet back in place as I use my weight to force the outer door closed. Henry completes the final maneuver. Both front and rear entrances to Grandma's workshop slam shut within seconds of each other, trapping DeKlerk inside.

"That's not going to hold him for long," Zach warns. "What's to stop him from pushing the cabinet aside and walking right through that door?"

"Good point. Help me move this tool bench. Stack anything heavy you can find on top of it. It's not foolproof, but it should hold him for now."

Sweaty and exhausted, Zach tries to catch his breath. Me, I'm functioning on pure adrenaline. I lift the garage door. Henry and Rebecca appear and join us in securing Grandma's workshop with everything we can get our hands on.

"I can't believe we just pulled that off," Zach says.

"How long can we hold him there?" Rebecca asks.

"Long enough. Those doors are solid. He'd have to make a pretty big commotion if he tried to break either of them down," I proclaim.

"What about his phone?" Henry asks.

"In his jacket pocket, if I remember," Zach announces. "The jacket he took off because it was so hot in the basement."

"We got this guy twice in as many days. So glad DeKlerk thinks he outmatched his formidable adversaries," Henry boasts.

"I don't want to burst anyone's bubble, but we're not in the clear just yet," I point out.

In fact, we're far from being in the clear. Henry and I have to get home. Zach has ten unanswered texts from his mom, who is probably moments away from calling the police. Rebecca has no idea where her grandmother might be. And then there is *Belmont Estates Senior Community*, not to mention all of the things we still don't know about Grandpa's past.

But there is something we have now that we didn't have a few hours ago—the paintings, the real ones this time. DeKlerk is neutralized for right now, but I have no doubt we'll be dealing with him again sooner rather than later.

"Everybody into the car," Henry shouts. "Answer your mother's texts before I get pulled over for kidnapping, Zach. Rebecca, I'll drop you at your grandmother's. Robbie, you and I need to get home!"

Chapter Twenty-Seven
Separation Anxiety

First, we drop off Zach, then Rebecca, and Henry and I are on our way home. Neither of us says much. The only plan we make involves the paintings. We have to remove them from the trunk of the car and get them up to our shared bedroom closet, a place no parent would look for fear of attack by falling objects.

Mom and Dad invite us to join them in the kitchen. They are planning something, but seem surprisingly relaxed. The half-empty bottle of wine and newly filled glasses offer some hope we might escape further interrogation. Just to be sure, I fill in the basic facts, minus a few key details.

"I picked up the package Grandpa left with Charlie."

"Thanks, guys," Mom replies. "What was in it, anyway?"

"We didn't open it," Henry interrupts.

"We locked up the house and left," I add.

"I think we've all had enough activity for one day, let alone one week," Dad suggests. "Tomorrow is Saturday. No work. No school. We'll have some time to figure out what's next for Grandpa. I assume I can count on you both to stay put for the rest of the night."

"No worries. I just have to get my stuff out of the car," Henry explains.

"Do you need any help?" Dad offers.

"I'm good. I'll be right back."

So far so good! Luckily the paintings are small enough to be concealed in Henry's duffel. I head upstairs. Henry follows a few minutes later. With our parents downstairs, we have time to find the space needed to hide the paintings, somewhere between Henry's hockey equipment and my collection of old cameras.

Task complete, Henry remembers he doesn't have his phone. Not only was Henry's phone the key to finding out about *Belmont Estates Senior Community*, but its absence also meant I pretty much had his undivided attention for the past few hours. But that definitely shifts as he realizes any attempt to leave the house is a no go, even for someone as clever as him.

It's sort of weird. This is probably the first time I've thought of Henry as clever and not just devious. I can't remember ever feeling like we were on the same side of anything before. I always wanted to look up to my big brother. But it was hard with him pretty much always putting me down. It's been different for a couple of days. It just doesn't feel like it's going to last. Let's hope his attention doesn't fade along with his bruises.

The next half hour passes in complete silence, with the exception of Henry tossing and turning in bed. No one is talking, but no one is sleeping either. Mom and Dad finally make their way upstairs. The only other sounds to be heard are muffled whispers and their bedroom door closing.

"I can't fall asleep," Henry announces.

"Me neither."

"I have to get my phone back. It was a good idea to leave it in DeKlerk's van when I did. But there are other things going on, and I need to get it back."

"Because of the fight you got into the other day?"

"Look, Robbie, we've helped each other out these past few days. But this is something you really have to stay out of."

Before he finishes his sentence, Henry is out of bed and peering through a small opening in the door. He slips into his jeans and sweatshirt, shuffles his feet into a pair of sneakers, and bends down to tie the laces.

"Are you crazy? It's midnight!"

"Exactly, and with any luck, I'll be back here before daylight."

"Where are you going and how are you getting there? And what if you're not back? What am I supposed to tell Mom and Dad?"

"Never mind. What I need from you is your phone."

"No way. You're about to take off and leave me with no way to contact you, Zach, or Rebecca?"

"I'm doing this one way or another. It's just that your phone makes it much easier and much more likely that I get back before Mom and Dad are awake."

Henry extends his hand; I unplug my phone. He sticks it in his back pocket, grabs his wallet, and makes his way downstairs. "He won't remember to turn the alarm off," I mumble to myself. I hold my breath, waiting for the piercing noise to wake the whole neighborhood.

Nothing, no alarm, no noise, no Henry, no Zach, no Rebecca, and once again, no phone! I look out the bedroom window and watch Henry disappear as he turns the corner. I stare at the clock on my nightstand, willing the digital display to advance, despite knowing that with the morning comes endless questions from Mom and Dad.

I can't tell them what I don't know. And I don't know where Henry is off to in the middle of the night. Zach probably is safely tucked in. Not knowing what is happening with Rebecca and her grandmother makes me a little crazy. The only thing that makes me less worried is that DeKlerk is nowhere near them for now. I have to stop thinking. I have to get some sleep.

Read a book—no way. I can't concentrate. Count sheep—people say that works. Not for me. Grandpa's remedy—warm milk and honey. I hate milk. Check the clock—12:08 am. I can't believe only eight minutes have passed. Watch a video—that should do it. Don't have my phone!

I can't put the lights on. That will surely alert Mom and Dad that something's up. Focus—but on what? Grandpa, DeKlerk, Rebecca, Belmont Estates, paintings. I wrap myself in the blanket and bury my head in the pillow. Morning cannot come fast enough.

Chapter Twenty-Eight
When You Least Expect It

Either I'm dreaming or Henry is lying across the room. Without knowing when or how, Henry slipped back into the house; his snoring confirms his presence and wakes me up. Unsure of whether it's been minutes or hours, I glance at the clock—5:35 am.

Whatever triggered Henry's midnight disappearance, he kept his word. I have no idea where he went or what he did. But he is back as promised, no small achievement for someone as unreliable as him.

I consider getting out of bed and checking on the package concealed in the closet. The assumption is that it contains the paintings, although come to think of it, that is not actually confirmed. I hesitate, less concerned about waking Henry than Mom and Dad.

With the chance of falling back to sleep zero to none, I scan the room to see if my phone returned with Henry. I spot it on the floor, barely noticeable under the pile of clothing he discarded before getting into bed. I twist around and extend my arm as far as possible, but my reach falls short of the target. Reluctant to move about the room, I make another attempt to retrieve the phone with the lace I pull from the sneaker under my bed. I fashion a loop just large enough to grab the phone lasso style. The first and second attempts fail. One more try. Got it!

So far so good. Henry is out of it, which for the moment gives me the opportunity to investigate a bit further. I check the recent calls. Nothing incoming, but a half dozen outgoing calls Henry must have made last night. All of the numbers are local; none of them are familiar. I still have no idea what my brother was up to with his mysterious vanishing act in the middle of the night.

"Playing detective, little bro?" Henry whispers from across the room. He sits up, yawns, and rubs the sleep from his eyes.

"Where were you?" I demand.

"Lower your voice, Robbie. You'll wake Mom and Dad," Henry warns.

"You're worried about me waking them up? That's a laugh, given your little escape routine last night. What kind of trouble are you in, anyway?" I insist.

"Given my history, I know the bruises and hiding out at Grandpa's don't exactly recommend me for Eagle Scout, but you need to trust me on this," Henry offers.

"Trust you to do what?"

"To get to the bottom of this whole business with Grandpa," Henry explains.

"I really counted on your help these past few days, more than I would have expected. But let's get real, Henry. Trouble is not just your middle name; it's your motto. I don't know where you were or who you called last night, but the last thing we need right now is to turn to the creeps you usually hang out with."

Henry is surprisingly silent during my outburst. He doesn't elaborate or defend his actions. He remains unusually calm and simply asks again that I trust him. The conversation, if you can call it that, comes to an abrupt end with a knock and Dad's appearance in the doorway.

"I thought I heard voices. How come you guys are up so early?" Dad asks.

When in doubt, or more like when you have no answer, turn it around. "What are you doing up, Dad?"

"Gonna go for a run with the dog before he starts barking and wakes Mom up," Dad replies. "When Mom gets up, we'll have some breakfast and figure out what comes next."

Dad exits. Mom is asleep. I give it another try and still come up empty. Henry is not revealing where he went or what he did overnight.

Before I have a chance to press him further, the texts sound off one after another. Both from Zach, *What's up?* Then, *Any news about DeKlerk?*

Henry looks over my shoulder, grabs the phone, and responds, *Need the video clip from Belmont. Text it ASAP!*

"Why Belmont? What's going on?" I interrupt.

"Because in about an hour, the police are going to show up there with a warrant to search the place."

"And DeKlerk?"

"My guess is he's been back there for hours," Henry explains.

"How did that happen?" I ask.

"Let's just say not everyone I know is a creep, and not every text I get is a drug deal," Henry continues.

149

"And now I suppose you will take off your glasses, pull out your cape, and leap tall buildings in a single bound."

"Close, but I don't wear glasses, little bro."

"Okay, forget the superhero reference. Just tell me how DeKlerk got out of Grandpa's basement and made his way back to Belmont Estates," I demand.

"I'm afraid if I tell you anything else, I will have to kill you," Henry jokes.

"Very funny, but you're not getting off that easily. And since Zach has his orders, what's next for us?" I ask.

"I'm working on that," Henry thinks aloud.

"Well considering Mom and Dad expect us to sit down to a warm, fuzzy family breakfast and work out a plan for Grandpa's rehab, I trust your superpowers will come up with something."

"There's more to those paintings we stashed in the closet last night. And the old man, sorry, I mean Grandpa, is probably the only one who can clear that up," Henry reasons.

"No kidding. And even though Mom and Dad know about Grandpa's childhood and stolen art, there's a lot more they don't know," I remind him.

"For some reason, Grandpa wants to keep it that way. I just don't get why."

"Me neither."

Luke announces Dad's return, bounding up the steps, and jumping on my bed. Mom wakes to the simultaneous sound of his bark and the ring of the house phone. Dad walks toward their bedroom. Curious about the caller's identity, we wait to see if we are off the hook for the family conference.

"It's Anna, Grandpa's nurse," Dad reveals. "Everything's okay, but Mom and I need to go to the hospital for a 10 am meeting to discuss the rehab plan. It looks like we're going to have to make some decisions sooner rather than later."

And there it is, the out we need, access to a car, and time to examine the paintings and check in with Rebecca. I can't figure out Henry's deal. Superhero or con artist? I guess the next few hours will tell.

Chapter Twenty-Nine
No News Is Not Always Good News

First things first. It takes Mom and Dad about a half-hour to get their act together. Coffee made, to-go mugs filled, bagels toasted, and they are off. "We'll call you from the hospital when we have a clearer idea of what's happening with Grandpa," Mom shouts as they exit the side door to the driveway.

The sound of the car's engine and the thud of the falling trash bins confirm their hurried departure. They also confirm the certain debate between them about who is a better driver and who should be behind the wheel when they are in a rush.

"My money's on Mom," Henry declares. "She is definitely a better driver than Dad and no one can beat her record when it comes to knocking down those trash bins!"

Command and control of this operation is clearly in Henry's hands, at least for now. Whatever went down overnight has not only made him more certain about his actions; it has made him almost funny.

"True, but since you set things in motion last night, would you care to tell me what's next for us?" I interrupt.

"The package, little brother! Let's get to it and see if it sheds any light on what DeKlerk is after."

It is no small feat to remove the items surrounding the three brown paper-wrapped packages. One false move and the contents of the entire closet will bury us. Hockey equipment pushed aside, I lift the box containing my camera collection. Henry carefully extracts the paintings and places them on the floor between our beds.

"Don't rip open the wrapping," Henry cautions. "We're going to take a look and reseal them until we figure out what to do."

My obsessive opening of birthday presents, determined to preserve the wrapping paper, finally pays off. Henry hands me a small pocketknife from his nightstand drawer. I methodically slip the blade under the tape and open the first package with surgical precision.

Henry assists as I slide the canvas out of the wrapping. We repeat the process a second and third time, revealing three versions of the same scene. Depicted in each is a landscape, a field of grass and scattered wildflowers, with a small cottage in the background. The difference in each is color.

"I'm no art expert," Henry declares. "And I don't know why anyone would paint the same thing three times, but I guess you could say there is something beautiful about them."

While Henry and I agree the paintings are beautiful, and maybe even valuable, we are no closer to knowing how they connect Grandpa to the Bauer family or DeKlerk.

"The paintings you found in Grandpa's bedroom, did they look like these?" Henry asks.

"It was dark, and I only had a minute before I shoved them back under the bed. Besides, I wouldn't know one from the other anyway," I reply.

"But DeKlerk is convinced the paintings under Grandpa's bed were copies. My guess is these must be the originals he was after." Henry interrupts.

"Is that what this is all about—swapping fake art for the real thing and ripping off the real owners?" I ask, still trying to understand the connection to Grandpa.

"We know DeKlerk is a crook, but this is not just about forged artwork," Henry declares. "There is something more to this. I just don't know what."

My phone dings with an incoming text from Zach. Attached is the video he took in the basement at Belmont Estates. Even though the images are blurred, and the lighting poor, a large collection of artwork is visible. Henry reaches for my phone, saves the video clip, and forwards it, certainly not to any of my contacts, but to an unfamiliar number he recites from memory.

"Who are you sending that to?" I ask.

"To the special agents who are about to conduct the search at Belmont."

"I still don't know how you pulled that one off, but what are we supposed to do in the meantime?"

"Call Rebecca. I want to be sure she has Grandma Bauer in her sights and nowhere near Belmont."

Following Henry's orders, I make the call. No answer. Just the accented voice of Lillian Bauer instructing me to leave a message. Once again, I freeze and do not leave a voicemail.

"Try Zach," Henry insists. "Maybe he's heard from Rebecca this morning."

"Nope, not since last night when Henry dropped her off at her grandmother's house," Zach reports.

Henry grabs my phone and enters the number he texted the video to moments ago. Whoever answers confirms the search of Belmont Estates is underway. DeKlerk is cooperating but insists he is the legitimate custodian of Belmont's residents and the artwork stored in the estate's basement. He is refusing to answer any other questions without his lawyer present.

"Get dressed, Robbie."

"Are we going to Belmont?"

"No. We need to find Rebecca and her grandmother. I don't like the fact that you haven't heard from her, not with DeKlerk on the loose after being sprung from Grandpa's last night."

"But he's at Belmont. You already know that."

"He's there now, but that doesn't mean he didn't take a detour before returning to Belmont."

"What about the paintings?"

"Rewrap the canvasses and put them back in the closet. We'll deal with them later."

Dressed and ready, Henry and I jump into the car, conveniently left behind when Mom and Dad went to the hospital. We drive clear across town in absolute silence, a remarkable accomplishment considering who is in the car. The one person we did make contact with, Zach, is not missing out on this ride along. His persistence outweighs

Henry's objection and so we pick him up on the way to Lillian Bauer's house, the last known location for Rebecca and her grandmother.

Chapter Thirty
Mr. Haraway

Haraway—why does that sound familiar? I know I've heard the name before but I don't remember when.

We arrive at the house where we last saw Rebecca just over 12 hours ago. Several texts while en route and still no response. When the phone goes to voicemail, Henry insists I leave a message. Yes, it is possible Rebecca no longer has her phone, but it is a chance Henry and Zach convince me is worth taking.

As we debate whether to leave a voicemail message, knock on the door, or simply wait to see if someone emerges from the stately Victorian home, a taxi pulls up in front of our parked car. The driver pops the trunk, removes a large suitcase, and opens his passenger's door. He offers the elderly gentleman his arm and escorts him up the steps to the covered porch. The driver carries the suitcase to the now seated man. The two chat for a moment, money is exchanged, and the driver leaves.

"Who is that?" I whisper.

"No clue. Let's see if anyone opens the door," Henry replies.

After catching his breath, the old man slowly rises from the chair, leans on his cane, and makes his way to the door. He alternately rings the bell and knocks on the door to announce his arrival, but no one answers.

"Looks like no one is home to greet the old guy, whoever he is," Zach announces.

"Whoever he is, we still have no idea where Rebecca and her grandmother are," I remind Henry and Zach.

"True! Looks like you're going to have to poke around a bit, little brother."

"I'll do it," Zach volunteers.

"Leave it to Robbie. I need you for something else," Henry orders.

I step out of the car and walk toward the house, careful not to startle the old man. He shuffles back to the chair he occupied a moment ago, undisturbed by my approach. In fact, he seems rather pleased to see me.

"My eyes aren't what they used to be, but my guess is you're John's grandson, the younger one," the gentleman announces.

"I am," I answer cautiously. "But how did you know that?"

"Well, if these new-fangled phones are good for one thing, it's the photographs your grandfather and I exchange every once in a while."

"You know my grandfather?"

"You could say that, young man. Indeed, we go back quite a long way. I suspect he has mentioned me on occasion. He certainly has told me a lot about you."

Henry and Zach look on anxiously from the car, hesitant to interrupt my longer than expected chat with the unknown visitor. Introduction over, I realize who the elderly man is. I am in the company of my grandfather's friend from the old neighborhood, the art dealer who lived next door to him in Brooklyn, Mr. Haraway.

The conversation reveals this is Mr. Haraway's second stop since arriving in the U.S. from Amsterdam this morning. When no one was home at Grandpa's, he instructed the taxi driver to take him to the next reasonable location, Lillian Bauer's home.

"I'm a little surprised to find you here, young man," Mr. Haraway offers. "I wasn't aware that you knew about your grandfather's connection to Mrs. Bauer, at least not yet. Although, judging from your presence, I presume John has decided to confide in you."

Caught off guard by this latest development and not knowing how to respond, I say nothing, hoping my silence invites further explanation.

"Where is John, anyway? I hadn't given him a precise date for my arrival, but he was expecting me sometime this week," Mr. Haraway continues.

"He's in the hospital. He had a stroke several days ago," I explain.

"Aha! Now I understand why I haven't heard from him these past few days. How bad was it?"

"Pretty bad. He has this thing called aphasia. He only says a few words and it's hard to have a conversation with him. But if you hang in there, you can usually figure out what he means."

"Can I see him?"

"I don't know, but I think we're getting a little ahead of ourselves," I reply.

"I realize you have no idea why I've returned to the States, what business I have with your grandfather, and where Mrs. Bauer fits into all of this."

"That's a good start because the only time I ever heard your name before was when my grandfather talked about the time he lived in Brooklyn."

Neither of us is willing to go much further, not certain what the other does and does not know. That signals a change in topic as Mr. Haraway asks about who is waiting for me in the car. Once I identify the cars' other passengers, he asks if we might help him find a place to stay.

"Might I impose upon you to take me to a hotel? I was hoping to stay with your grandfather, but under the circumstances, a hotel will do just fine."

"I'm sure we can help you get settled somewhere. How long are you planning to stay?" I inquire.

"That will most certainly depend upon your grandfather."

Just when I am about to take my questions to the next level, Henry and Zach step out of the car, unable to contain their curiosity any longer. They make their way to the porch and are introduced to Mr. Haraway. Henry is in no mood for small talk and polite chatter but stops dead in his tracks when Mr. Haraway asks if we might make a brief stop at Belmont Estates before taking him to a hotel.

As Henry, Zach, and I assess just what this request means, another taxi pulls up in front of the Bauer home. This time, the driver removes a wheelchair from the trunk, and carefully positions his passenger onto the seat. When he sees the gentleman step down from the porch to greet Mrs. Bauer, the driver returns to his vehicle and takes off.

"My goodness, it's been years, Herbie. What are you doing here?" Mrs. Bauer asks.

"I planned on phoning once I was settled at John's, but I've just heard he's in the hospital," Mr. Haraway responds.

"Indeed, terrible business, getting old. I do hope he makes a full recovery. Perhaps we might both visit him now that you're back in the states."

"Well, aren't these two cozy with each other," I whisper to Henry and Zach.

Reunion with Mr. Haraway complete, Lillian Bauer expresses only a little surprise at our presence. "I suppose you young men are looking for Rebecca," she announces.

"We were hoping to find her here," I answer, cautiously.

"I'm afraid that is quite impossible. Judging from the time, my granddaughter is now safely aboard a flight to San Francisco to be reunited with her parents."

Chapter Thirty-One
Brooklyn

I have been to Brooklyn twice in my life, both times with my grandfather. The first time was six years ago for my grandmother's funeral. I was seven years old and there was a big debate about whether I was too young to attend. Mom, Dad, and Henry were there too, of course. Henry would have skipped the ritual if given the chance. I was determined to attend and never left my grandfather's side. The second time was a much happier occasion. We did a quick drive by his old neighborhood on the way to Coney Island. I was nine, and Grandpa insisted I sample every possible amusement park ride and boardwalk delicacy.

Two possibilities. Henry, Zach, and I prolong our stay at the Bauer house, or we leave. It is just not clear which will shed more light on the connection between Mr. Haraway and Mrs. Bauer, or Mr. Haraway and Belmont Estates. Our window of opportunity is shrinking with the certainty that Mom and Dad will be looking for us any minute.

"You are not staying in any hotel, Herbie. I won't have it," Mrs. Bauer exclaims. "With Rebecca no longer here, I have more than enough room. I insist. I will have the housekeeper make up the guest room for you when she returns from her errands."

"That is most generous of you, Lillian. I'm not particularly fond of hotels and promise not to be a bother," Mr. Haraway replies.

Despite our growing curiosity, we decide to leave. We have lost an invaluable source, Rebecca. We need to focus on what Henry's contacts have discovered about DeKlerk and what Rebecca's absence means.

Once back in the car, Henry learns the search of Belmont is complete. Files have been removed for further examination of their authenticity. For now, however, DeKlerk's claim holds up. He appears to be the legal custodian of the art collection. And none of the residents or staff report unusual or suspicious activity.

"You mean breaking and entering and holding us hostage isn't enough to put that crook away?" Zach shouts.

"I don't know, guys. DeKlerk has been pretty aggressive, but is it possible Rebecca has this wrong?" Henry questions.

"There's only one way we're gonna find out," I insist. "I've got to get back to Grandpa."

I call Mom. The meeting with the social worker has just ended. Grandpa is going to be discharged to a rehab facility in the next several days. She has to go over the list of facilities with him to decide which is best. Then they wait for a bed and hope they get their first choice. Yes, Henry can drop me off at the hospital to visit. No, he can't hang on to the car. Dad needs Henry to help organize things to get Grandpa ready for the move.

"Where does that leave me?" Zach asks.

Before anyone can answer, two dings. Incoming texts arrive on both Zach's and my phones.

"It's Rebecca!" we call out at the same time.

"How can you send a text when you're in the air?" Henry asks.

"She's not in the air," I reply and read the text aloud. *Never boarded flt to SF. Where r u?*

"You or me?" Zach asks.

"Let me," I answer. *Strange visit with Grandma. Who is Herbie Haraway?*

Rebecca continues. *No clue.*

"Ask her where she is," Henry demands.

I do, and she replies. *Brooklyn! Can you meet me?*

Me again. *What's in Brooklyn?*

Her reply. *Too much to explain. Can u get here?*

We go back and forth several more times. The only thing I determine is Rebecca has new information from something she found at her grandmother's last night. She texts a photo of a note with an address in *Breukelen*.

"Let me see that," Zach says.

"What is that word?" Henry asks.

"It's the old Dutch spelling for Brooklyn," I answer.

"What else does it say?" Henry and Zach ask in unison.

"It's hard to make out from the photo. It looks like another Dutch word. I think it says *poppenhuis*, and there's a signature, *Nathan*," I answer.

"Tell me the address. I'll google it," Zach offers.

"3033 Surf Avenue," I answer.

Zach keys in the address on his phone. Henry enters it on the car's navigation system. They both agree. It is

Brooklyn, Coney Island to be specific, about an hour and a half by car from here.

"There's no way we can get to Rebecca now. Mom is expecting you at the hospital, and I've got to get the car back to Dad," Henry reminds us.

"But there's a train that will get us to Grand Central. I'm sure we can figure out how to get to Brooklyn from there," Zach chimes in.

"That could take hours. We can't just leave Rebecca stranded all that time," I insist.

While we debate strategy and frankly come up empty, Rebecca texts another photo, this time of a sign above a building, **ANTIQUE TOYS & MEMORABILIA**.

For some reason, the sign seems familiar. I stare at the photo for several seconds. "I remember that place," I exclaim. "Grandpa took me there. He said he had to meet someone."

"Who?" Henry asks.

"I don't know. The guy never showed up," I utter softly.

"Do you remember a name?" Henry persists. "Think!"

"It was a long time ago. Wait, I do. Bauer, it was Nathan Bauer," I blurt out, stunned at my own words.

Chapter Thirty-Two
Antique Toys & Memorabilia

It was more than four years ago. I was nine. Grandpa took me to Coney Island. It's a vague memory, but a good one. I was totally preoccupied with rides and food, but I do remember the stop at the antique toyshop. I remember the shop was closed when we got there. I remember that we waited for a while, but the man never showed up. I remember the name, *Bauer*!

"We've got to get back to the hospital," Henry declares. "Whatever is going on in Brooklyn will just have to wait."

"Not necessarily," I interrupt. "We, I mean Henry and me, we have to get back to the hospital, but you don't, Zach."

"Okay, where are you going with this?" Zach asks. "And what am I about to do that I know I'm going to regret?"

"I figure Rebecca took a huge risk not getting on the flight to San Francisco. We need to take an equally big risk and find out why. Something she learned between the time we dropped her off last night and the time her grandmother whisked her off to the airport this morning made her take an enormous chance," I think aloud.

"You know, my grandparents still live in Brooklyn. Let me think. It's a long shot, but I might just be able to come up with a way to get to Rebecca," Zach proposes.

And he does. Not only does Zach have a plan to take the train into the city, but his grandfather agrees to meet him at Grand Central. From there, they'll take the subway to Brooklyn, where Zach will stay overnight. Zach's parents are delighted. His grandmother has already started cooking. And here is the best part—there are fireworks in Coney Island tonight to celebrate the summer solstice!

Zach resumes the texting blitz with Rebecca. *On my way!*

Her response. *Robbie too?*

Then Zach. *Just me for now. Will get to my grandparents by 3 at the latest.*

Rebecca. *Meet me at the toyshop at 5.*

Zach again. *What will u do till then?*

Rebecca. *DK. Need to check some things out!*

This is the third time in as many days Zach has taken over with Rebecca. Despite my doubts, there have been no major blunders. Let's hope he is three for three!

After a brief stop at his house, Zach and his backpack are on their way to the railroad to catch a 12:40 pm train, due into Grand Central at 1:50 pm. Henry and I arrive at the hospital. Mom gives me the go-ahead to visit Grandpa. Dad reclaims his car along with Henry.

The thought of being separated from Henry, Zach, and Rebecca for the next several hours is worrying. Let's just hope the decision to divide and conquer pays off. The strategy—divert, stake out, question, regroup!

If all goes well and a bed is available, Grandpa will be discharged to a rehab facility within the week. Of the five that are most highly recommended, two are actually in Brooklyn.

"It's a schlep," Mom says. "But if it's the best place for Grandpa to recover, Brooklyn it is!"

"So he won't be living with us?" I ask.

"Maybe for a little while after rehab. But the team is pretty optimistic. He's starting to communicate fairly well between speaking and writing. It's not always clear, but it's coming along. If they get him up and walking, at least with a cane, he should be able to manage at home with therapy and a part-time aid," Mom explains.

Grateful for the news, I give Mom a hug and proceed to Grandpa's room to size things up for myself. This could be the break I need to get some answers about DeKlerk, Haraway, the Bauers, and of course, the paintings.

His syllables a bit garbled, his smile still skewed, Grandpa is not just happy to see me. He actually seems relieved. He is no longer confined to bed. Still attached to the monitoring equipment, he is seated, a blanket over his lap, a notepad and pen on the adjustable table to his left.

Mom remains in the room at first. She is not offended at Grandpa's request to have some time alone with me. While he doesn't exactly ask her to leave, his suggestion she gets herself a cup of coffee is loud and clear.

So many things have happened in the past few days, I don't know where or how to start. Fortunately, Grandpa takes the lead. The spoken sentences are strained and broken into short bursts. The frustration is obvious, as he loses a word and searches to find it. He looks away, embarrassed, yet determined to continue.

I remind Grandpa about the notepad. Although awkwardly formed with his left hand, the written words begin to answer my questions. One by one, Grandpa answers.

Do not trust DeKlerk.
Lillian does not know.
Three paintings.
Haraway will help.
Find Rebecca.
She can find out.
Coney Island.
Toyshop.

The pieces come together. Although the words don't give me much new information, they do confirm things. But I still don't know why. Why has Grandpa denied having a brother? Why all the secrecy about his past? Why does Rebecca know more about my grandfather than I do? There is also one big what—*what can Rebecca find out?*

Grandpa's sadness is unmistakable. None of this was supposed to happen this way. He lost the chance to tell the story on his terms. He apologizes over and over again, not so much with words or gestures, but with his silence. I take his weakened right hand in mine, and we sit in that silence for several minutes.

The interruption, at first unwelcome, is exactly what Grandpa needs. His melancholy shifts to determination. I read the text from Rebecca aloud. *Waiting for Zach at*

Antique Toys & Memorabilia. Owner thinks she knows your grandfather!

Chapter Thirty-Three
Hidden in Plain Sight

I'm not sure all redheads are fearless, but there is no doubt about Rebecca. She knew she couldn't get on that flight to San Francisco. She also knew her only chance of dodging her grandmother was the airport. As long as she had a credit card and some cash, she could get to Brooklyn from JFK.

It was a little tougher for Zach to convince his grandparents to head to Coney Island four hours before the start of fireworks, but he did. They were delighted Zach planned to meet a friend there and teased him only slightly on learning the friend was a girl.

I get a few more bits of information between Grandpa's occasional dozing and the nurses' checks of his vital signs. When Mom returns, the notepad is hastily concealed. Once again, and for reasons that remain unclear, Grandpa holds tightly to his secret. And the centerpiece of that secret is unquestionably linked to the antique toyshop in Coney Island, Brooklyn, New York.

I step out of the room, presumably to use the toilet in the hall, but actually to see if Rebecca and Zach have made contact. Text successfully delivered, I see Henry and Dad approach from the bank of elevators in front of the nurses' station.

"Mission accomplished!" Dad exclaims. "We packed a suitcase for Grandpa and checked things out around the house. He's good to go whenever they discharge him to rehab."

Dad's announcement makes me a little uneasy. I don't know exactly what his checking uncovered. I am mostly concerned about what he might have seen in the basement given the chaos of DeKlerk's brief capture last night. I take comfort in the absence of any questions and Henry's relaxed state. Of course, that could just be drugs, but hopefully not.

"Are you high?" I ask, with Dad out of earshot.

"Actually, I am, but not on drugs," Henry declares.

"What's going on?"

"I listened to Grandpa's voicemails when I was at the house, the ones on his home phone."

"Where was Dad?" I ask.

"Packing up the car," Henry assures me.

"And?"

"And, there was a message from that Haraway guy," Henry explains. "He knows about DeKlerk."

"Exactly what does he know about DeKlerk?" I ask. "Grandpa thinks Haraway can be trusted, but can we really be sure?"

"I don't know, but there were two other messages—from someone at the antique toyshop in Coney Island," Henry continues.

"What did he say?"

"It wasn't a he. It was a she," Henry corrects me.

"Okay, what did she say?"

172

"First of all, she called Grandpa, Mr. Bauer. Then she asked about the paintings. And then she said something I didn't understand, about *poppenhuis*."

"What about her second message?"

"She was surprised she hadn't heard from Grandpa since Josef DeKlerk had already contacted her."

"I'm calling Zach. Why hasn't he answered my text? He must have hooked up with Rebecca by now," I conclude.

Mom appears in the hallway, no doubt curious about my prolonged bathroom break. Surprised to see me chatting with Henry, she smiles and steps back into Grandpa's room. A moment later, Matt Russo, the speech therapist, approaches on his way to visit Grandpa.

"Your grandfather is doing quite well," Matt proclaims. "He's using a lot more words and the writing is really giving him confidence."

"You remember you translated **WEES** for me? Has my grandfather used any other Dutch words?" I inquire.

"What did you have in mind?" Matt questions.

"Did he ever say or write the word *poppenhuis*?" I ask.

"Not that I recall. But I actually know what that means," Matt offers. "It means dollhouse."

Indeed, it does mean dollhouse, not just according to Matt Russo, but also according to Zach and Rebecca. I finally hear from them. They have met Eva Groff, daughter of Emile Groff, the original owner of Antique Toys & Memorabilia. The younger Groff tried to reach Nathan Bauer for months. When she learned of Nathan's death, she undertook the search for his brother, John.

While Zach is unable to come up with any good reason to cut the visit to his grandparents short, Rebecca is on her way back from Brooklyn. Cell service is a bit erratic as she waits for the 8:20 pm train in Grand Central, but the meaning of *poppenhuis* is confirmed. What's more, it is not the paintings themselves DeKlerk is after. It is the dollhouse.

"What's the connection between the paintings and the dollhouse?" I ask.

"The paintings depict some sort of message or conceal a code needed to open the dollhouse," Rebecca explains.

"I don't get it," Henry says, as he listens over my shoulder.

"Have you unwrapped the original paintings yet? Did you notice anything unusual about them?" Rebecca asks.

The conversation ends abruptly as Mom becomes increasingly suspicious about the length of time I spend with my brother and away from Grandpa. Matt exits and I take his place alongside Grandpa's chair. Henry picks up my signal. He invites Mom and Dad into the hallway. I get Grandpa to myself, but for no more than a minute.

Luckily, that is all it takes. I remove the notepad and pen from the table drawer.

In response to my first question, Grandpa writes— poppenhuis.

In response to my second question, he writes—Look at the colors.

In order to open the dollhouse, we have to make sense of the different colors of the three paintings. When Henry picks Rebecca up at the train station, she confirms what we have yet to figure out. What do three paintings, identical except for color, hidden in my closet, tell us about opening a dollhouse? What does a dollhouse—possibly stored for decades in an antique toyshop—reveal about my grandfather's past?

Chapter Thirty-Four
Assembly Required

Rebecca was scheduled to arrive in San Francisco within the hour, 7:30 pm local West Coast time, 10:30 pm here in New York. Instead, she is at Grandpa's house—Henry's idea, not mine. With Rebecca settled for the night, Henry calls my cell.

"Are you nuts?" I ask my brother. "Aren't her parents expecting her?"

"Not anymore. She convinced them Grandma Bauer had the dates confused, and she would be arriving next week, after the school year is over," Henry explains.

"And they bought it?"

"Apparently," Henry confirms.

"What about her grandmother? Where does she think Rebecca is?" I probe.

"As far as she knows, Rebecca landed in San Francisco a half hour ago. Rebecca figures Grandma Bauer is fast asleep by now and doesn't expect to hear from her granddaughter until morning," Henry continues.

"And then what?"

"We cross that bridge when we come to it. One step at a time, Robbie," Henry says reassuringly.

"Okay, so what's our next step?" I ask.

Henry instructs me to sit tight. Rebecca has other news, information that could help us make sense of the paintings and their connection to the dollhouse. The paintings are not to be viewed individually. They represent something called a *triptych*, three paintings to be viewed together and assembled in a certain order. It is the order that reveals the paintings' message about the dollhouse.

"Rebecca knows this how?" I question.

"Eva Groff, the current toyshop owner," Henry offers.

Only when Henry puts Rebecca on the phone are the remaining details evident. It is not now, and never was, the paintings DeKlerk was after. Emails retrieved from her grandmother's computer last night revealed DeKlerk's intentions and the reason for Rebecca's sudden mission to Coney Island. For him, the prize is the dollhouse, an antique of tremendous worth. That is what he told Rebecca's grandmother while persuading her that no one else's claim to the treasure other than hers was valid. She alone should benefit once the dollhouse is found. Of course, he never would have shared anything with Lillian Bauer.

Henry returns home at midnight. It is well before his typical Saturday night curfew, and early enough not to provoke our parents' concern. We have eight, possibly nine hours until Lillian Bauer expects to hear from her granddaughter.

Mr. Haraway is temporarily sequestered as Grandma Bauer's houseguest. Zach is still in Brooklyn, which is most convenient. Surveillance at Belmont Estates, which my brother has arranged somehow, indicates DeKlerk has not left.

We move around the room as cautiously as possible, lighting our way just enough to remove and unwrap the paintings for the second time. They have to be placed in a specific order. I stare at the individual canvasses, hoping for some hint about how to assemble them.

"I don't have a clue. How are we supposed to know what goes first, second or third," I whisper.

"There are only six possibilities," Henry reminds me. "The trick is figuring out if one order makes any more sense than the other five."

We go at it for almost two hours. Is it the progression of colors between canvasses? Is there an image that becomes more obvious with one order versus another? Does it help if the paintings are turned upside down?

"I need to get some sleep," Henry concedes. "We've got to put this to rest for now. Let's pack things up and take a fresh look in daylight."

I set the alarm on my phone for 5:30 am. This time of year the sun will be up well before Mom and Dad. But that is not what wakes me. I get a text from Rebecca at 4:10 am. *Can't sleep. Regenboog—its Dutch for rainbow. Look for a rainbow.*

Henry is sound asleep, snoring peacefully. I don't know how he does it, but at least one of us is keeping his cool. I open the closet and step inside. I close the door, turn on the light, and position myself in a small clearing between hockey equipment and never hung up clothing. I recall that of the various combinations of canvasses we examined last night, one seemed to progress from red to orange to yellow to green to blue to indigo, and then violet, R O Y G B I V, a rainbow.

"Wake up. I think I have the right order," I loud whisper. "And that's not the only thing I found."

"What else did you find?" Henry asks, his words muffled by a simultaneous yawn.

"We never looked at the backside. With the paintings assembled in this order, if you examine the backs, where the canvasses are tacked to the wood frames, there's a word spelled out, scratched into the wood. I think it's a name," I explain.

"What name?"

"I think it says Rivka, R-I-V-K-A," I reply.

"Whose name is that?" Henry asks.

"I think it's a Yiddish or Hebrew name, English translation, Rebecca or maybe Eva."

With sunrise and full daylight, things get even clearer. Luke barks and this time, both Mom and Dad decide on an early morning run with the dog. The paintings, now disassembled, are safely back in the closet. Henry and I fake the sleep we both could use until we are certain they are at a sufficient distance from the house.

We phone Rebecca to alert her about our success at assembling the *triptych* and our discovery. Rather than surprised, she seems vindicated.

"Rivka, is that Yiddish or Hebrew for Rebecca?" I ask.

"It is, but it's not me," she answers. "I've known for months that our grandfathers were brothers. But now I know what Eva Groff told me yesterday at the toyshop must be true. There was a third child, a girl. Our grandfathers had a younger sister, Rivka Bauer. The dollhouse was hers."

Chapter Thirty-Five
Over the Rainbow

The last kindertransport left from a port near Amsterdam in the Netherlands in May 1940. My grandfather and his older brother, Nathan, were aboard with 72 other children. They were taken to England where they were met by authorities at Liverpool Station in London. They never saw their parents again. Their younger sister, Rivka, only three years old at the time and too ill to make the journey, was taken in and hidden by Gerta and Jakob Groff. Rivka's name was changed to Frida to erase any remnant of her heritage. She grew up alongside the Groffs' son, Emile. In 1958, at the age of 21, Frida and Emile were married and immigrated to the United States.

"It's an incredible story," Rebecca declares, after revealing what she learned from Eva Groff.

"How does it fit with DeKlerk's claims?" I ask.

"It doesn't. Even though he acknowledges a sister, DeKlerk denies my grandfather had a brother," Rebecca reminds us.

"And, why do you think Eva Groff is believable?" I ask.

"Because there were references among my grandfather's papers to the family members he lost during the war. He wrote about his parents and a young sister. He was convinced his only living relative was his brother, your grandfather," Rebecca explains.

"But if he thought his sister was killed along with his parents, what makes you think she survived and somehow ended up in Brooklyn?" Henry interjects.

"Two things," Rebecca declares over the phone. "First, we know DeKlerk is after the dollhouse, not the paintings themselves. That's why he's been to the toyshop in Brooklyn, presenting himself as the executor of Nathan Bauer's estate, and his widow Lillian Bauer's attorney. Second, wait a minute. Before I tell you the second thing, let me text a photo of Eva Groff I found on the toyshop's website. See what you guys think."

The phone signals the text's arrival, and once again, I see the spitting image of my mother, not as a child, but a full-grown adult. It is not just the red hair and freckles, but the distinctive way she half smiles while biting her lower lip.

"This could be Mom's sister," Henry says.

"But she's not. She's her first cousin," Rebecca explains.

"I think I got it. Grandpa not only had a brother. He had a sister. His sister's daughter, Eva Groff, is my mother's first cousin, right?" I attempt to clarify.

"And my father's first cousin too," Rebecca declares.

"I guess that makes sense," Henry acknowledges.

"And Eva Groff, your mother's and my father's first cousin, is in possession of the dollhouse DeKlerk is after!" Rebecca exclaims.

"I'm still missing a few pieces. How did Eva Groff get the dollhouse?" I persist.

"It was the one family treasure the Nazis didn't get their hands on. When Frida came to America, she brought it with her," Rebecca continues.

"So how did DeKlerk find out about it, and why did he insist he was after the paintings?" Henry interrupts.

"That part is still unclear, but I think it has to do with something your grandfather told him," Rebecca replies. "DeKlerk was after the paintings, but not because they were of any value themselves. He believed he needed them to make the exchange and access the dollhouse."

Rebecca's phone signals an incoming call. No surprise there. Grandma Bauer is trying to track her down. She puts me on hold just long enough to dispel her grandmother's worst fears.

"What did you tell her?" I ask.

"It's not what I told her. It's what she told me," Rebecca offers.

"I don't get it."

"She was actually relieved I hadn't gotten on the plane. Something that Haraway guy told her has made her wary of DeKlerk, finally. I don't know what he said to her, but she wants me to meet with him as soon as possible," Rebecca continues.

Mom and Dad return from their run, which rapidly ends the call. I stare at Mom, still amazed at all the redheads suddenly turning up in my family. Henry gives me a not-so-gentle nudge. A leisurely Sunday breakfast is not an option. If Rebecca is meeting with Haraway, I want to be there.

Time for a bold and risky move. Henry looks at me as if I am out of my mind, but it is a chance worth taking. I ask Mom if Grandpa ever mentioned anyone by the name of Haraway. After a moment's hesitation, she recalls my grandfather's old friend from Brooklyn.

"Grandpa hasn't mentioned him in years. Why are you asking?" Mom questions.

Henry senses I have no clue where I am heading and comes to the rescue. "When Dad and I were at Grandpa's, I listened to his messages. There was a call from someone named Haraway."

"Strange, after all these years," Mom wonders aloud.

"Well, he's in town," Henry explains.

"Maybe he could visit with Grandpa," I jump in.

"That might be a good idea," Mom agrees. "Let me check with Grandpa."

By early afternoon, everything is in motion and everyone is accounted for. Mom and Dad check out a local rehab facility. Zach arrives from Grand Central. He convinces his parents to let Henry and me pick him up at the station. Rebecca, having had a pretty restless night at Grandpa's, waits anxiously. With our foursome reassembled, we head to the Bauer home.

What Grandpa found too difficult to disclose over the decades and struggles to communicate since the stroke, Mr. Haraway reveals in less than an hour. Grandpa and Nathan Bauer were, in fact, brothers, separated first from their parents and younger sister, and then from each other. With fewer foster families than refugee children, the boys were placed in an orphanage outside of London. Nathan, eight years Grandpa's senior, broke his promise that they would return to Amsterdam after the war to find whoever and whatever was left of the family. Instead, when the opportunity arose, Nathan left for the United States in 1946.

That pretty much sealed the deal for Grandpa. Abandoned by his brother and convinced that no other Bauers survived, he changed his name to John Robert Orphan. In time, he too made his way to America.

"Just like the famous song," Haraway says. "We all expected our dreams to come true once we made it over the rainbow."

"Did they?" I ask.

"For most of us, yes. But not without sacrifice, and for your grandfathers, tremendous loss. John never forgave Nathan. Nathan never forgave himself. Even when they discovered their sister Frida, I mean Rivka, survived the war, their joy was brief. While they were only children themselves, each, in his own way, lived with enormous guilt for leaving her behind," Haraway explains.

"How did they find out their sister was still alive?" Henry asks.

The answer to that question connects the rest of the dots and casts Mr. Haraway in the leading role. Of the several priceless *poppenhuisen*, or dollhouses, believed stolen by the Nazis during the war, one was never located. It made its way from Amsterdam to America in 1958 with Frida Groff, aka Rivka Bauer. Mr. Haraway, a well-known art dealer and appraiser, was contacted by Eva Groff two years ago, after her mother's death, to determine its value.

Meticulous research revealed the dollhouse's authenticity, as well as its provenance. It also uncovered the story of the Bauer family and led to the identification of three rightful claims of ownership—Eva's mother, and her uncles Nathan Bauer and John Robert Bauer, aka Orphan.

Coincidence or irony, John Robert Orphan and Herbert Haraway were old friends and shared many stories about their lives decades ago, both before and after the war. Haraway heard of a brother's abandonment. He heard of a sister, believed to have perished during the war. He heard of an exquisitely crafted dollhouse, given to the young girl on her first birthday. He even heard of a set of paintings, a triptych, on whose wooden frame the brothers carved the letters of their sister's name, R-I-V-K-A. Only when she placed the three canvasses in the correct order and spelled her name, did her brothers let her play with her favorite toy.

"But that was just another story until it wasn't. It was just another story until DeKlerk entered the picture," Haraway recalls. "He knew about the one missing dollhouse from the antique collection in the Netherlands. He believed it was brought to America in the '50s, and that in all likelihood, no one realized its value."

"How did he make the connection to my grandfather?" Rebecca asks.

"DeKlerk was presumably in the business of determining rightful ownership of art stolen during the war. He offered to assist Nathan in recovering what once belonged to the Bauer family. Instead, he enriched himself wherever he found an opportunity," Haraway confirms.

"Once he started digging into the Bauer history, DeKlerk was convinced of two things. First, there was just the kind of family estrangement he could manipulate to his financial advantage. Second, Eva Groff, her mother's surviving heir, had no idea of the worth of the dollhouse."

"But she did know, didn't she?" I ask.

"She did after she contacted me," Haraway assures me. "And thus the plan to distract and delay DeKlerk was devised by your grandfather, Robbie."

"The plan?" Henry, Rebecca, Zach, and I utter in unison.

"Indeed, the very plan John, no doubt, would have confided in you, if not for the stroke," Haraway concludes.

It turns out the paintings don't hold the key to the dollhouse. But they did send DeKlerk on a pretty wild goose chase, which is just about to come to a deadend.

Chapter Thirty-Six
In His Own Voice

"Resentment is a powerful force, Robbie," Dad explains.

"Retribution may be even more powerful," Mom adds.

To put it into Henry speak, *Payback is a bitch.*

Awful, unspeakable things happened to millions of people during the war. Some of these things were beyond anyone's control and were born of pure evil. Others arose from cowardice and deceit, or, in Grandpa's case, from unfulfilled promises.

What I know now, three months after Grandpa's stroke and finally in his own voice, is that the loss he suffered grew each year. He created a new family, Grandma, Mom, Dad, Henry, and me. But he cut himself off from the one person who shared his pain. He cut himself off from his older brother, Nathan. And while he took some comfort in knowing his young sister survived the war, he never saw her again or met her daughter, his niece.

Grandpa told wonderful stories, and I was usually the beneficiary of his tall and often humorous tales. But he frequently told half-truths, not to deceive, but to conceal the hurt. Whether prompted by Rebecca's appearance last June, or DeKlerk's plan to con Lillian Bauer by insisting that he and Nathan knew each other only as friends, Grandpa decided I would finally know the whole truth.

The details Grandpa disclosed, confirmed by Mr. Haraway, gave Interpol—the police authority that investigates international crime—all the evidence it needed. Assisting with the inquiry was the art fraud division of the FBI, alerted to DeKlerk's activities by undercover operative Henry O'Neill. Yes, in the world of nothing is as it seems, my formerly drug-addicted, twice thrown out of school brother is working undercover for the Drug Enforcement Agency, commonly known as DEA. His law enforcement contacts and the evidence Grandpa and Mr. Haraway provided will likely put DeKlerk away for decades.

Henry leaves for school tomorrow, where he plans to continue his studies in forensic science or something to do with crime scene investigation. I have my room back, with a closet I promise to eventually organize.

Rebecca's family, including Grandma Bauer, and mine finally have met and exchanged histories. They expect to complete the move to San Francisco in another week. I'm not sure about Mom and Dad, or Henry, but I expect to see the Golden Gate Bridge in the very near future. I know for sure Zach will accompany me. He has a pretty huge crush on my new cousin.

Grandpa is graduating from rehab and will live with Mom, Dad, and me, at least for a little while. His speech is not always clear, and he still searches for words. The notepad comes in handy from time to time, particularly when he gets emotional. And that seems to happen more often these days. But whether he speaks or writes, it is always his voice that I hear.

"A brother is a gift, boys. Take good care of each other," Grandpa says.

"We will," Henry and I reply simultaneously.

The only unfinished business and decision we leave to Grandpa is whether he would like to meet his niece, his sister Rivka's daughter, Eva Groff. He agrees and asks that she visit him at our house once he is settled.

Henry and I arrange to pick her up at the train station the following week. As we drive to the house, Eva's anticipation, as well as ours, is evident. We exchange some polite small talk during the several minutes it takes to get to the house.

Despite the warmth of the late September afternoon, Eva's hands visibly tremble as she fusses with the car door handle. Henry mistakenly lowers the cars' windows instead of unlocking the doors. I trip in my rush to help Eva out of the car. Everyone clearly is nervous.

No need to ring the bell. Mom and Dad are standing in the doorway, equally anxious to meet Eva Groff. At first, the greeting is reserved, but an enthusiastic round of hugs quickly follows.

We are a bit more cautious about Grandpa, uncertain about his reaction to his sister's daughter. He is hesitant at first, but his smile, still skewed from the stroke, and his grasp of my hand as he slowly rises from the sofa tell me he is ready for this moment.

Mom's eyes are fixed on Eva Groff. She is astounded at how much she and her cousin look alike. "Where does the red hair come from, Dad?" she asks.

"I don't remember so much, but I do remember Rivka's hair," Grandpa sighs.

The conversation is polite as we learn about each other. Grandpa does his best to retrieve memories from his childhood in Amsterdam. He is understandably reluctant to speak of the separation, the London orphanage, and his journey to America.

He does ask Rebecca if there are photos among her grandfather's papers. Rebecca recalls having seen a few and promises to go through everything again.

"I don't have any photos, but I brought a video, Uncle John. Is it okay if I call you Uncle John?" Eva hesitates. "I made the video about a month before my mother died."

"I want to see it. Please," Grandpa whispers.

With that, Eva produces a clip on her phone. It is her mother, Grandpa's sister. Her hair is no longer red. She half-smiles as she bites her lower lip. She proudly displays her dollhouse, inviting the viewer to enter its miniature rooms. There is not a dry eye among us as our families are introduced to Rivka Bauer and listen to the story Grandpa is finally able to complete.

CPSIA information can be obtained
at www.ICGtesting.com
Printed in the USA
BVHW041213070121
597279BV00009B/121